In Beautiful Shadows

In Beautiful Shadows:

The Sunrise

Lady Trish

authorHOUSE®

AuthorHouse™ LLC
1663 Liberty Drive
Bloomington, IN 47403
www.authorhouse.com
Phone: 1-800-839-8640

Published by AuthorHouse 08/12/2014

ISBN: 978-1-4969-2131-4 (sc)
ISBN: 978-1-4969-2129-1 (hc)
ISBN: 978-1-4969-2130-7 (e)

Library of Congress Control Number: 2014911273

Contents

Acknowledgments

I'm so grateful to my husband Jean-Carell Desert, who encouraged me to create my blog (beautyofconsciousness.wordpress.com) a few years ago. Since then I have been more than encouraged by the fervent readers who never cease to write on Facebook or send me encouraging messages to keep on writing. I will never forget Mr. Stepha Pierre, from College Le Phare administration, to whom I entrusted my first fifteen poems written in my algebra notebook when I was in ninth grade; he believed in my ability and always reminded me to never give up writing. I am grateful for the wonderful Stephanie Sainvil, who has read and counseled me on all of my previous attempts to write this novella- She's just amazing! My heart is filled with thankfulness for so many other people who personally shook my idleness in finishing this novella. To cite a few: my mother Junelle, my great aunties Bedlyne & Erlande Milien, "l'infatiguable" Levy Alexandre, Evely-love D. Glemeau, Nina Snemyr Kringlen, and many other readers who remain close to my heart. Thank you, guys. I Love you.

Prologue

It is ten o'clock at night, and the laughter from the street is echoing in my head, crumbling the wall in my small bedroom. The twin bed has not changed after five years, and it's still firm on the ground. There is no private room where one can reside to clear thoughts that have been suffocating somewhere for so long. This house has turned into the most pitiful place: the beautiful beige wall has been washed and rewashed for fingerprints, and the chandelier in the living room is missing a few crystal balls. For a two-story house with six bedrooms, one would think the people living around here would realize its value and try to uphold a reputation in the neighborhood. But I guess not. A motel seems a better idea than renting the second floor with the nice balcony where I contemplated jumping off many times. But let's be real: a few missing teeth is all I would get. Not much height for a suicide.

These drunkards outside still won't shut up, and they will be there until three in the morning, ruining any chance I have of resolving my insomnia. I need some fresh air; the breeze outside is much more appealing than leaning on my back on this old mattress and thinking about things I wish I could do. This bedroom is a prison with no lock on the door; it has three windows, one facing the front yard and the other two directly facing the bedroom of my dear voyeur neighbor. He knows when my lights go on and off. He knows when I cannot sleep, and he can hear every word of any conversation going on in my bedroom. Recently, he heard my older cousin Ninnie nagging me because some low-life liar told her that I kissed her sixty-five-year-old boyfriend. Some people are determined to stay ignorant. What purpose could I possibly have in hanging out with an old guy who has nothing but long, nasty teeth and barely deep pockets? The thought of kissing him makes me sick. Ninnie was supposed to be the so-called responsible adult with whom I live, but in reality she is the kind of lady who loves money too much to do anything good with it. She used to be so good to me during my first few weeks of living with her, but everything is going downhill nowadays. She taught me a lot, but I guess she got tired of taking care of other people's kid. I'm just another inconvenience on whom she discharges her anger every time she is broke. I used to like her so much, but she is another example of how people can never be trusted.

This house is so full of people that it's impossible to breathe at night. The nice white ceramic floor can never stay that way with so many dirty feet coming and going. There are feet from after a soccer game, the ones from a quickie away from their wives, the ones hiding from their husbands, the ones who just got brutalized by their boss, the ones dragging from exhaustion after a home-clinic abortion, and the ones escaping after stealing the last fifty dollars that were going to feed everybody in the morning. Not to mention the noisy neighbor who comes in to observe and concoct rumors afterward. I am starting to think adultery is not such a bad sin because I don't see anybody around here getting any kind of punishment for it.

There is nothing to do. I don't feel like writing any stupid poems tonight. I jump off the bed, walk past the damaged living room, get some water out of the well, and take my clothes off to shower in the middle of the paved backyard. This professor that lives in the street behind the house couldn't ask for a better view; all he has to do is install his chair on his terrace and observe the anatomy of the many young women that take their showers in my backyard. The broken, sophisticated shower room was of no use, and frankly I love taking my shower out here in the open. I really do not care about the neighbors enjoying this view; tonight I am not going to hide in any corner to shower. I pull my towel from the hanging line that has been tied up even before I was conceived, and I wrap it up around my chest and then dry my feet on the carpet before going back in the house—a routine not many people around here learn to do. I pull a white T-shirt from the basket of clean clothes and dig deeper to find a denim skirt. Now I am ready for some fresh air.

The breeze is brushing my skin, and the shadows of the palm trees are drawn in the brick wall of the lined-up houses. It would be a great, serene summer night if it weren't for the strong smell of tobacco mixed with pure sugar cane liquor from the shack next door. Men are like roaches in the street. There goes my fresh air. I do not want to go in their direction—not tonight. I do not want to feel their devious eyes watching my every step, calling me names, and whispering gossip I've already heard. It is a custom, and none of them ever miss a meeting. Even when they are broke, they still sit at the bar begging passersby for money to pay for their liquor. I fed one of them once, and I will never do it again. I was at the bistro buying my sandwich when he asked me for five dollars because he was starving. Out of pity I gave twenty dollars, but all I gained from that were rumors that I was interested in him. As if! They are all gangs of dropouts still living at their parents' house; the more advanced ones may have a high school diploma. Drinking and bad-mouthing girls is like the full-time jobs they will never have.

I stand in front of the house observing the meli-melo going on in the street, and it takes me back to three summers ago—a summer night forever written in my brain-journal like a bad tattoo after a drunken night. No one knows about it, of course, and it is going to stay that way. People around here are always giving new twists to stories, so I'll probably die with this secret.

The banker across the street notices me in front of the house. I can see his eyes undressing me from my denim skirt to my camisole tees. He wipes his rugged, dry lips with his tongue and waves at me. I look at him from head to toe and turn my back, ignoring his gesture. Even with a decent job, he is still repulsive. He has small, funny eyes; goofy cheeks; a flat forehead; small hands; and a medium, fat stomach. I cannot stand him anymore. Whenever he comes from work, he will wave at us from this balcony, chat a little, and then close his door. He will come out until later in the afternoon, every day with a different woman. I never see him talking loud. If I'm not in front of him, I can barely hear what he's saying, and he always looks like a suspect for something. He once went on a date with my cousin Linda, and she took me with her as a chaperone, to assure the adult of the house that nothing would happen. Some crap!

I do not know why some parents still fall for these acts. Folks in this town consider it respectful if one is going to one's boyfriend's house and take another person with as a chaperone, supposedly for the sake of preserving dignity. If anyone asks me, it is bogus. The chaperone job is not easy; it requires patience, and the reward for not telling had better be great for the welfare of every party included. As a chaperone, I have seen hands under skirts, detached bras, and kisses that lead to me waiting patiently for hours. The night Joe took my cousin Linda on the date, he was wearing a white shirt unbuttoned at the top, revealing his crucifix necklace hanging over his nasty chest hair. French songs were playing, and he was smiling and whispering words to Linda. He was sitting behind the wheel like one of those machos who thinks he has it all under control. In the meantime, I was sitting in the back and trying to look distracted, to give them their privacy. He was driving on the boulevard, and the wind was a little strong. I don't know what went wrong with his little Toyota from 1900, but the *bobotá*[1] stopped right in the middle of the road. He was a banker who lacked the money to put gas in his car before taking a girl out. I bet he only had the hotel money in his pocket. That night I actually felt bad for him as he got out of the car to push the car in the rain with both of us inside. The rain was gradually increasing, and about five minutes later, we could hear the water hammering on the car like a big knock on a door. I was a little worried, but when I noticed the look on Joe's face, I found the situation hilarious. I sustained my laugh because I didn't want him to feel embarrassed while he was trying to turn the engine back on. He leaned back on his seat, scratching his flat forehead, and I could tell he was extremely nervous. Then he got out of the car, and for a moment I thought he was going to leave us there and run. But I thought, *he lives right across our house, so he wouldn't dare do such a thing.* He started pushing the car so that we could have a chance of going back home without having to wait hours for a tap tap.[2]

Linda looked at me, and I was not sure whether to laugh or be sympathetic. "I think we should help him somehow," I suggested.

Linda stared me down and replied, "Are you serious? Sit your butt down. We are not helping anyone." She was pissed and at the same time shamelessly laughing at Joe and his car. "He should have known

---

[1]   Something useless

[2]   Common cars used for transportation in Haiti

to fix his *bobotá* before proposing to take me out. I am not getting out in the rain—hell no." He couldn't smile at Linda anymore because he looked like a dead chicken fresh out of hot water. There was a dead silence in the car, and nobody wanted to break it. He managed to reach the gas station five minutes away, and after he filled his tank, he drove us right back home.

That was before three summers ago happened. Every time I turn to the blank pages where my teardrops formed a few shallow marks, I envision the whole scene. I swore to myself that I would keep these pages until I got some answers. It has been three years now. Although going back to my teardrop art on the old, blank pages saddens me, I just want to keep them there. I cannot bring myself to tear up these pages. Not now, and maybe not ever. Sometimes I even forget what really happened; it feels like a bad summer dream. It feels like one of those nights when it is too hot to fall asleep. I cannot cry anymore. Nowadays I feel like laughing about the whole situation.

The Apple

It is our border.
Once eaten, we can never go back.
Gruesome words,
Once pronounced, can never take back.
The apple is evil, pure evil,
And since Adam,
Men have sworn to be one.

Part One

Chapter 1

It was about eight o'clock. I rushed into the house, hiding my eyes with my hands so that nobody could see that I'd been crying. I passed Ninnie sitting with her friend on the patio. She said, "Hey, young lady, where are you coming from at this hour?"

I acted like I didn't hear what she said because I didn't want her to see me. I rushed upstairs, sat on the floor on a dark corner, pressed my hands over my mouth, and started crying. I bit my hands and my clothes. I wanted to scream. I felt so dirty, so ashamed of myself. I sat there crying with my knees up against my stomach. I rocked my body back and forth against the cold wall. I wanted to knock my head really hard and die. My heart was racing inside my body; I was hot one moment and then cold the next. I was sweating because I'd cried so hard. I felt a sharp pain in my belly, only it wasn't really physical. My mind was speeding at a thousand miles per hour, asking all kinds of questions to which I didn't have the answers. I couldn't talk, and my tongue filled up my mouth like somebody was suffocating me. I was on fire. I lay on the ceramic floor, flat on my belly, so that I could ease the pain. I squeezed my belly with one hand, and the other hand covered my cries.

Then I stopped, turned on my back, looked at the ceiling, and said to myself that it was nothing. That it did not happen. That tomorrow it would all go away. I stripped off my underwear and painfully walk my way downstairs. I took my clothes off with such a rage and threw them on the floor. I poured water on me and started scrubbing my skin like I wanted to take a layer off. I kept scrubbing and scrubbing, but the smell was still there. I covered myself with soap and washed my body multiple times until I became so weak that I had to stop. I rinsed my body and threw my clothes in the trashcan.

I slid under the one heavy blanket on my bed, covered myself from head to toes, and tried to sleep. Every time I closed my eyes, I saw his face. I tossed and turned in bed, but it was as if I could feel him all around me. I could smell him and his cold, heavy hands on me. I could see his flat face with a half smile looking at me. I was helpless, and that night I thought I was going to die. I grabbed my notebook and tore the pages where I'd drawn flowers and butterflies. Then I grabbed my pen and tried to write. I couldn't. My tears ruined every page I turned, and my hand was shaking so hard that I couldn't write a thing.

I sat down, my feet on the cold floor and my hands supporting my head as I leaned forward. I wanted to cry but couldn't find a reason to do so. I checked the time, and it was only two o'clock in the morning. *One day a tall, dark angel will push me against a brick wall and passionately kiss me. Probably he'll hold my small waist with his strong hands and lift me up afterward, to kiss my neck. He will look at me through the halo of the moon and smile as he positions my spine on the green of a mountain, like he's offering my body as a sacrifice to the gods. Then I will smile as the adrenaline of the uncertainty alerts my sense of the danger that might surface in the near future. Nothing like a little bit of danger to make everything feel right.*

I kept rocking my head against the wall, as if my thoughts were not a strong enough drug. Six o'clock in the morning found me soulless and lying on my stomach on the ceramic floor. I never made it back to the bed.

"Are you okay, Dara? What is it with you sleeping on the floor? You'd better not be pregnant, I'm telling you. I see you've been hanging out with that tall boy. He'd better be using protection!"

"What?" For a moment I thought I was dreaming, but when I heard the click-clack of Ninnie's sandals in the hallway, I knew I was back in hell.

"Excuse me? What makes you think we are doing that?" I replied, half awake with my journal still in my hand.

"Oh please, you think you can fool me? This guy wants nothing more but to use you and go back to his normal girlfriend."

Wow! So I have to be the girl who is being used instead of the girlfriend a guy would proudly have? I opened my mouth to tell her that just because she is giving it away to a married man doesn't mean everybody else around her is doing the same. But I foresaw a whole month of tension and crude arguments, so I swallowed the pill, smirked, and ignored her comment. I watched her as she swirled her thirty-day-old weaved hair and walked away with her long, skinny legs. *God give me the strength not to hate that woman!*

"Good morning, Dara," whispers my creepy neighbor from his window. "You got to bed really late last night."

"I guess it was not just me," I replied, leaving the bedroom before he could say another word. This guy started to really creep me out.

If he says one more word to me today, I swear ... "This house is a nightmare," I mumbled low enough so that he wouldn't hear.

It would be redundant to have a local newspaper when one could just step outside and ask the reporter next door, "Hey, what's going on today?"

"Oh, last night one of the guys said he saw Lila kissing the Big Boss, who always drives his big Mercedes late at night. We always suspected them to be together, but nobody had proof. But tonight there will be lot of drama because the Big Boss's wife heard the news."

I wonder who told her, I thought to myself while trying to look distracted so that Mousy didn't read my expression. Anything I wanted to know, I could ask him. Mousy got his name because of his pointy nose and lips. Mousy was about my height, but he was so skinny that I wondered whether he ever ate. He was very useful, always running errands for someone in the neighborhood.

"And by the way," he added just before leaving, "there are rumors that the president might not live to see the end of his term again. There have been a lot of attempts to shoot him or burn the palace altogether."

Mousy really didn't have to fill me in on that last detail. Who cared if the president got shot? As much as I loved this beautiful island, I wish it had never been discovered—then maybe we wouldn't be having one selfish government after another. Those *prétendu* intellectuals need to take their suits off and go under a few palm trees, drink some coconut water, and dive in the beautiful beaches and leave the country alone.

I kinda liked Mousy, though. Last week he told me to be careful with the guys drinking by my house late at night because one of them might have suggested doing "certain things" that he could not, for the sake of his life, reveal to me. But I was not afraid of the "certain things" this guy was planning. Mousy did not tell me which one of them, but I had an idea who, and he was not so tough. The idea of me fighting in the dark for my life while he was doing something I would probably enjoy really entertained me—or would I fight back? *I wonder what he would say if I visited him tonight ...?*

At sundown, I slid a pair of white jeans with a sateen lace top for the sake of hiding something. I sat down on my bed rethinking my decision, but the look on his face had been too vivid for me to miss. I did not even bother fixing my curly, stubborn hair in the mirror; I was sure it would pass for a style. I walked past Ninnie's room, and her married boyfriend glanced at me through the half-open door. It took a few second to unlock my eyes from his because I could not believe the expression I read on the pervert's face. I wanted to wave and say, "Hey, perv," but I gave him the most honest smile. I did not know how I did it; I just did. Maybe someone else resided deep inside me, and she was better off there because the world was wicked enough.

Minutes later, I stood in front of the wooden door and breathed before I knocked. Junior opened the door, and I felt so satisfied when his jaw almost hit the floor. There it was. I did not say hi—I waltzed my way in the room by gently removing his hands on the doorknob. "I heard you said you wanted to rip me apart," I said as I turned around and faced him with the most inquisitive stare.

"I-I'm not sure what you mean," he barely mutters before swallowing a mouthful of saliva.

"Well, Junior, I don't know how to say this, but your wish will be a reality tonight." I took a deep breath, smiled, and walked one step closer to his face. "Junior, I would like for you to rape me."

Dream Me

Dream me nude with
Your repulsive mind.
Rid me of that decency I
Dreamt of passing on.
Color me red with your
Devious eyes.
Undress that puritan I
Rerouted a while back.

Touch me softly, hard enough.
Erase the feel
That confuses
My senses.

What an awful bliss,
Needing something one is yet to master!
Beauty of danger!
It was never love, I'm told later.

Chapter 2

It would be easier to predict a volcanic eruption than Junior reading my eyes and predicting the minutes afterward. I stood in the middle of the room facing the window where I caught him watching me undress so many times. I turned my back to him and let my posture own his whole space. Who would have thought that sixteen years ago, some mother somewhere would give birth to such a distraught girl? I was insatiable for things that would probably never make any sense.

"I beg your pardon?" Junior said.

"You beg my pardon? Who would have thought you could articulate such beautiful a expression without muttering …"

"Are you high on something?"

"That is more like it. But no, I am as alert as you can get, and if you are not interested, well, I can always leave. No hard feelings." I started for the door.

H-hold on, wait. Why would you want me to do that?

"You mean besides fulfilling your wishes?"

"*My* wishes?" he repeated.

Junior stuffed his hand in his pockets, trying not to look through the garment that softly flared the lines of my figure, but that did not hide it enough. He would probably give in the next few minutes. He looked at the ceiling like he was looking for answers or affirmation that this time he was not looking through his window. I was right there, a few inches away from him, readily offering what he had fantasized about for so long. I smiled as I moved past him and reached for the door.

He pulled me away from the door, locked his sweaty palms around me, pressed my chest against his, and kissed my lips—a kiss I disdainfully refused. *I guess another one bites the dust. So long, reasoning.* He pushed me on the bed, and I bounced a little. He hurriedly took my jeans off like he did not want me to change my mind. He really had no idea that I'd spent my whole afternoon planning this moment to the last detail. I'd seen it all unveiling before I knocked on his door, but somewhere in my wasted brain I was kind of hoping he would say, "Dara, find someone your own age. Get out of my room right now. I will not do such thing." But of course who was he to reason with his head? He was just another proof of the mistake Eve made by not poisoning Adam instead.

He squeezed my thighs so hard that his five fingers were stamped on my skin like on a sponge mattress. I could feel the blood rushing out of my veins after every stamp he created. As he was fooling around with my body, grabbing everything he could and leaving his saliva all over, I fixated on the ceiling with the coldest glare. *What does he think he's doing?* My eyes could ice Junior's blood and leave him stranded with the most disappointing feelings—but why on earth would he notice that? He was so occupied with his back and forth, sweating and breathing like a wounded goat and asking me if this was how I liked it. I was unmoved; he did not notice that, either. A few seconds after, he quivered like a bad earthquake, and then he blasted on his back and exhaled.

"Wow. Is that supposed to be it? I don't feel right." Somewhere in my mind I had thought that this must be good, otherwise why would everybody around me want it so much? They cried for it. They begged for it, got beaten for it, and some even took it without asking for permission. I was on my back and on this bed with someone who has probably been thinking about this moment since the day he noticed a few growths on my body, yet the intensity I'd heard about it was not there.

"Well, everything feels right over here. I have no idea what you're talking about, girl."

"Maybe you felt something, but I didn't."

He became defensive. "Are you trying to make me feel bad? Because that's not going to work. I did not force you to do anything."

"Why didn't you? That is what I asked for."

"You know what? You are crazy. I never took you for someone like that."

"Hmm, really? Is that why you think it would be nice to 'rip me apart'?"

"I never said—"

"Can you get me some water?" I interrupted.

"Sure."

He brought me back a glass of water and stepped out, probably to call a few friends and brag about his victory while it was hot in his blood. I left before he came back.

Midnight finds me scouring my eyes out in silence. It was one of those moments where I needed to clean my soul. My eyes turned red as I kept forcing out the tears. My heart was overstretching, but the ducts around my eyes wouldn't work. It was incredible how the human body worked yet still could be useless to emotions, as if for some undetermined reason, the mind is in another dimension. Please do not get me started on this whole duality; it never really comes in handy in real situations.

I hate my bed—disgusting bed. I really cannot believe this guy actually touched me. I should just slash an artery and wash the darkness out of me. Why didn't I feel the same way? Why did I ask him to do that to me? Now everybody is going to know, and I am so screwed. What is happening to me? How can someone agree to rape you and not do it right? I do not understand why I feel so bad. This should feel normal, right? I think that I may have sent him the signals to trap me. But why didn't Junior get it right? Maybe I should try not to think so much about sending signals. Maybe that is the problem.

Nothing was right about this night. The Big Boss's wife came to the neighborhood and screamed the hell out of Lila. Everybody stood forming a semicircle and watched the fight. Some were laughing and commenting, and some were impatient about what might happen next. The wife was plump with fair brown skin and short hair; a dragon tattoo way too large for her back made her neck appear even shorter. Any grown woman who was not afraid to leave her house at this hour to question a concubine has way too much free time on her hands. She was wearing shorts that caused her thighs to look even heavier. She was talking loudly, dancing around with her words to attract more audience, and screaming Lila's name. "This fake Limenna[3] needs to leave my husband alone, or I'll have her throat!"

Lila never came out; she was probably afraid because rumor had it that the Big Boss's wife had stabbed a few other women who were fooling around with her husband. Eventually, around two o'clock when things returned to what was the usual level of drunkards on the streets, everybody else went back to their homes. It was not like I was going back to sleep right after that. Of course, these kinds of scene always made everything more interesting around here. Every day it was the same boring routine, so it was almost like we were all impatiently waiting for a time when someone would have enough and start throwing a few bottles and rocks, or knocking on somebody's door to collect their cheating husbands. I don't know why women bothered with these men. It was almost like the wives and the husbands enjoyed these back and forth exchanges. The married jerks felt important because they had unoccupied wives to come fighting for them. Luckily, nobody came knocking at this house—yet. I liked to entertain myself with the thoughts that the people I lived with cheated with another level kind of men. Men whose wives did not care enough to generate any type of ridiculous commotion on the street, or who were educated enough to wait for the husbands to come back home and close the door before they trashed their stuff and made them sleep on the couch.

At least now there was something else that would reroute my thoughts and rock me to the land of nowhere. *God knows I can use the distractions.*

---

3   Bougie-like female.

Early the next morning I woke up to the scream of a lady next door. I looked through my window, unconsciously waiting for Junior to somehow come to my window and fill me in on what was happening. But who was I kidding? He would probably stop stalking me after last night. My pajama shirt was still unbuttoned, I held it closed with my hands and ran outside to see what was going on.

"Hey, girl, did you hear?" Mousy said.

"Hear what, Mousy? What is going on this early?"

"Junior is dead."

"What?"

"Yeah. At least you don't have to worry about him lurking around waiting to rape you."

"Rape me? Oh, that's what he said?" I tried to compose myself so that I wouldn't give away any clue that I was probably the last person to have seen him alive. Although I could care less how he rendered his last breath.

"He didn't exactly say it like that, but he sounded like that because I know there is no way you would agree to even kiss that guy. You would die before anything like that happened … right, Dara?" Mousy looked at me like he knew something that I did not tell anyone. Some part of me told me he was asking this last question on purpose; if anything happened in this neighborhood, he should know. After all, he was the reporter.

I decided to join in his little game, or whatever it was. "The irony is, Mousy, he went before I did."

"Yeah, and they found his body cold as ice early this morning. Somebody probably poisoned him, because there was no sign of bleeding."

"Oh, you saw the body?" I asked.

"Of course I did."

After he described to me all the crude details about how they'd found Junior's body, how people guessed he was probably still talking on the phone when he'd died, how his pants were halfway down, and all the other details, I got distracted and switched the conversation to something even more futile. Eventually the conversation lost its purpose, and there was no going back to bed for me. I headed through the front door and went straight up for a cold shower. Then I went on the terrace. I dragged a weak wooden chair and sat with my legs resting on the cold cement of the three-inch wall that framed my balcony, and I contemplated the whole neighborhood. That was my favorite spot, and the view was beautiful, although it was tarnished by everybody passing by and rushing to Junior's house with the excuse of supporting his family. *I am not going to wish condolences to anybody. It's not like I would mean it.* For every ten people who went to a bereaved house to wish condolences, six of them were enjoying the opportunity to satisfy their curiosity about the family's life or what the house looked like.

The green of the mountain slowly faded under the amber shadow of the sun rising. A few birds tweeted their way around, happy to have another beautiful day. *This is still not a good day, though. And Junior is dead? I still can't wrap my head around that. I mean, it's not like his existence meant something for the neighborhood, but ...* While I was diving into my thoughts, Joe came out of his house sneaking a woman (different from the one yesterday) from his bedroom. The woman turned around to kiss him on the cheek, but he was more focused on getting her out of there. The woman wore a miniskirt that shows off her nice legs, and she had on a shirt too tight for her bust. She adjusted her hair for the fifteenth time and fast-walked her way out of Joe's house. *Oh my God, is that Cece? She is fifteen! What a bastard! Why didn't he die instead? Maybe fate will take him next."* Joe raised his head in my direction and licked his lips. *Is that supposed to be a sexy look? He probably murdered that poor girl in there, and of course she is not gonna tell.*

He said to me, "Hey, beautiful, that is a very risky way to sit up there. Aren't you afraid to fall on your back? Be careful, ma belle."

As if I was known to be afraid of anything that might destroy me. A whole chain of events came unrolling in my mind every time he faked a hello to me. *Is he for real?* Maybe if the authorities were not too busy receiving bribes from the *zuzu* of the middle class, who think because they can afford certain privileges act like they own half of the world, this despicable animal would be rotting in hell right now. *Look at him, smiling like he gets some kind of thrill every time I ignore anything he says.* Even on the terrace, it was difficult to breathe. Joe closed his front metal door and turtled his way to his house, and all I could think of doing was throwing a nice big rock at his car parked in front of the house. *Maybe it's best to wait until tonight, when everybody goes to sleep. It will make me feel so good to see his face looking at his most prized possession in ruin. This neighborhood makes me sick.*

Everlasting

There is that kiss,
The soundscape love.
A quiet kiss
Like the feel of the breeze,
So pure.
Eases deep into the soul,
Travels the navel line
Till heart sheds tears.
The instant harmony
Of two lost souls
Drowned in the waves.

Chapter 3

In about one hour, a few friends from the school were going to come pick me up so that we could go to the beach and talk about a bunch of nonsense—of course men related. In about one hour I was going to know who slept with whom and what girl was the shared blanket these days. I dragged myself out of bed and tried to find something to wear. I had been up all night listening to music and trying to forget everything that had happened the day before, although Ninnie and her friends were not making it easy. Apparently some Diaspora is in town, and I heard one of her friends already had a contact number to invite him over the house for dinner. Of course she would invite him to this house, because she couldn't possibly have dinner with him and her husband at the same table. They talked for hours. I turned up my music, revoking any stupid interest I may have had to listen to the whole conversation.

From miles away I could hear my friends' laughter in the street invading the neighborhood. "Daraaa, let's go!" These girls had no respect, screaming my name like I lived far up a mountain where they couldn't walk.

I yelled, "I am coming."

Ninnie heard their voices and came in my bedroom while I was still in my two-piece and trying to find a dress to wear. "Where are you guys heading this time?"

"To the beach."

"Which one?" As if she saw a car parked outside, and we were going to drive one hour to the other village.

"We're just walking to *La Brise* to have some fun. We'll come back in about four hours."

"I will be in the area later on to see a friend, so you girls behave."

Seriously? She really wanted to play that card? I chuckled at the thought, grabbed my bag, and muttered a good-bye.

Outside, Jessica, Bianca, and Marise were impatiently waiting, popping their gum with hands on their waists like I had made them wait for two hours. "What took you so long?" asked Marise as she grabbed my forearm and dragged me away from the porch.

"I couldn't find something to wear."

Jessica said, "Oh please, girl, you could have come out with only your swimsuit, and it would have been just fine."

"Thanks, but I think I can wait till we get to where the swimsuit is intended for."

They all laughed. A few whistles were thrown our way, and the wind did not help us hide anything. We may as well have walked in the street with just our bathing suits on, like Jessica had said. We walked on the sidewalk and went past the café where a few guys were playing dominoes and screaming their points with certain authority. The one losing was always seen painfully wearing about twelve pincettes around his jaw, standing until he could actually win a round to earn his seat. When they saw us, they twisted their necks, winked, whistled, and asked if they could join us. My eyes caught a woman sipping on her manioc juice and shaking her head at the reaction of the fools sticking their tongues out and doing all kind of disgusting gestures while we passed by.

We crossed the busy intersection and caught the eyes of a few drivers as well. Men around here would get out of their beds for this sole purpose. Some were known to dress up nicely and stand on the corner by the streetlights, studying women passing by and selecting their date for the night.

We stopped at the bakery to buy patties and fresh croissants. From afar one could smell the different flavor of the breads and the cakes. The smoke was spiraling from behind the small house and evaporating in the air, which reassured customers that the bread was coming out of the stove right now. It was always so crowded in there, but that did not discourage us from leaving because everybody knew the wait was well worth it. An old lady in her seventies managed the bakery, and her staff consisted of her daughter and her two grandsons who had no choice but to put young ego aside and be the cashiers, school or not. I already knew what I wanted: two patties, and that would be all. Then I saw Bianca ordering two dozen patties and bottles of lemonade, and I had to ask who was going to eat all that.

"Oh, I invited a few friends to join us at the beach," she said waving her hand dismissively like it was nothing.

"Oh really? And when was I going to learn about these 'few other friends'" When we got there?" I asked, glaring at all three of them for not warning me. But really what I was worried about was for not going for my other swimsuits and maybe opting for denim short instead of my ridiculous white cotton dress.

Jessica looked at me and gave the most mischievous smile. "You look fine, honey." She kissed my cheeks and shrugged.

"If you say so."

I could smell the salty waves and hear the echoes of clashing water. It was the perfect time of the day to go to the beach. We were practically stomping our way over the steep hill because we were eager to jump in the water already. I noticed Mousy climbing the coconut tree right below the hill. I ran there, whistled at him, and asked him if he could peel one and bring it to me by the beach. "I don't know where I'm going to find a hatchet, but I'll see what I can do," he said. Of course I knew that meant a yes. I couldn't remember the last time I'd asked him a favor which he'd refused. He was like the messenger boy everybody would send for their dreaded commission, and I never heard him complain.

"Thank you, Mousy."

I wanted to pull my dress off the minute I got there, but then I remembered the girls invited guests, so I wanted to see what they looked like before running to the water like a lunatic. We chose the cleanest rock we could find and settled there. Marise placed the brown box with the patties on the rebellious grass growing in between the rock and waved at a few guys walking in our direction. I turned around and recognized one of them: he was tall, and I had spoken to him one time. It was the guy Ninnie claimed would only want to use me as a closet girlfriend, although I think what she was aiming for was a sex buddy. The other three were cute but too boyish for my taste. This tall guy had shoulders on which I dared to dream of resting my cheeks. I could not remember his name, but I figured I would know it in a few seconds.

Jessica jumped on the one with the round face and sweet dimples and kissed him like she wanted to eat his lips. *I guess this one is her boyfriend, then.* After he put her down, she swung around with a laugh and said, "Girls, this is my boyfriend, Jake." I don't know why girls change their voices around cute guys; it is ridiculous how they can go from a deep bass to soprano in a few seconds. She twisted her fingers and pointed at the one with the green cap and the nerdy glasses. "This is Stoner." *Oh yeah, of course. I could have guessed that name myself. I mean, who comes to the beach ready for research at the library?*

She turned around to the one already feeling Marise's rear end. "This is Marco, and this one is Sebastian."

"Nice to meet you all," I said while waving and not focusing on Sebastian, hoping that he forgot who I was.

"Hold on, I know who you are," he said, squinting his eyes like he couldn't recognize me clearly. "You borrowed my last *Blake* novel and never gave it back."

"I've been known to steal cowboy novels," I replied with a smirk.

"Well, well. Nice to finally meet you again, Dara."

Oh wow, he remembers my name! Jessica probably told him whom he was meeting in advance—no need to get ahead of myself here. He probably has one of those fancy, girly girlfriends who will never be caught wearing flip flops.

All of a sudden all my wild spirit left me, and I felt uncomfortable taking off my dress. Everybody dove into the patty box, and it instantly turned into a couple's retreat. Marise romanced with the macho who couldn't keep his hands to himself, and Bianca was trying to hold her composure while Stoner would not stop talking. I glanced at Sebastian, and he was already looking at me, so I looked behind him like I was just checking on something else.

At that moment, Mousy brought me my coconut. "Thank God for you, Mousy." I gave him a patty, and he left—probably on his way to peel another coconut for somebody else. I cracked the head and drank the delicious water with my eyes close, savoring every second of that moment.

A green leaf detached from a branch and floated right by my shoulders, and I was startled, leaving me with sugary coconut water all over my face. Sebastian laughed. I couldn't help myself and started laughing with him. Then he said, "This is what you get for drinking it all by yourself."

The girls took their clothes off and ran to the water, and I did not wait a second to do the same. Nothing felt better than floating on these waves that gently rocked me offshore and lured me deeper in the water. For a while I stayed on my back and embraced the sweet light escaping from the blue sky. It was so beautiful at the beach that it was mindboggling how some people would want to destroy every good thing left in this country.

Walking back to my house was heartbreaking. The girls had made me laugh so hard today. I wished there was a back door that opened to another street so that I wouldn't have to face any of those fools sitting around by the bar. When we got to the intersection, the girls had to go their separate ways. I hugged them good night, and Sebastian insisted on walking me to my door, but I firmly refused—though I really wouldn't mind hanging out with them another time. Sebastian hugged me last and kissed me on the forehead, and the girls started singing "La Vie en Rose" and laughing. I dismissed them with my hand, pulled myself away from him, and walked away without looking back. Right before I opened the door to my house, Mousy came to me, handed me a piece of paper, and walked away. I looked at him and then at the white neglected paper, which had come from his sweaty palm. *That guy is so weird.* I smiled and shook my head as he walked away without a good night gesture.

I felt the bliss in discreet, wishing

Another you and me—never again.

I blame across the street for your cold heart.

Wise men would say, though,

Choose the one that won't hesitate to kill for you.

Chapter 4

Once again I found myself between two rivers of feelings. It was almost like crossing the river with Moses holding his miraculous staff, yet wondering if I was dreaming or about to die. That forehead kiss … and to think that it was my first. I cannot remember whether, before my parents abandoned me, they used to shower me with forehead r cheek kisses, but as far as I can remember, that was my first forehead kiss. It was not the kind of kiss one received with the implied connotation, "I really don't care about you, I just want the cookie." No, this one was real and pure.

I could not make up my mind and figure out what was going on with Mousy, though. He had been acting really strange today. I simply placed his memo in my fresh-smelling, new journal and decided that nothing was going to get in my way of a good sleep tonight. I changed the clean sheet on my bed as if that would change the fact that I was still in this house. I turned on the radio, laid on my back, and stared at the ceiling. I'd found a lot of solutions while staring at this ceiling. But I was not looking for solutions tonight—I needed more of a clear idea as to how to understand my day. First I went to the used-to-be dreaded routine of reviewing the whole day in my head: the girls, the beach, Mousy, the incident with the coconut, Sebastian's eyes catching mine, his smile when I ran like a child in the water, his pondering look as he leaned on his elbow with his strong legs vertical on the dying grass, the smile on the corner of his lips when he handed me my towel coming from the beach, his silence as he graciously locked his index finger with mine while we walked, his offer to walk me to my door, and a forehead kiss to seal it off.

Through the open window, the breeze through the palms trees whispered their bliss all around my bedroom. I switched the radio to the jazz station. Music was a crucial part of this night, and everything was perfect. Then I realized I was not starring at the ceiling, and my eyes had been closed for a good period of time. It was only ten o'clock, and already my body was letting go. It was like I was still in the water and floating in between the strong waves. The last thing I remembered was the sensual voice of the man on the radio saying, "It is five minutes after ten, my dear audience, and I hope you are all enjoying our show tonight. Let the music relieve the stress of the day ..."

I remember smiling and thinking, *Dear, there was nothing stressful about my day.*

"Daraaa! What is going on with this girl sleeping at this hour of the day?"

I heard Ninnie's voice far away and repeatedly calling my name, as if I was passed out and she was trying to revive me. I had a chill as if I was in some kind of danger, so I opened my eyes, and the first thing I noticed was the wall facing my bed. At first I thought the house had crumbled down, and I had not heard anything. Then I checked around and saw the floor. *What? I'm sleeping upside down? How come I see the floor instead of the ceiling?* Strange things happened around here. I checked the clock, and instantly my mind woke up when I saw it was 11:30 AM. Then I turned around and found that I was on my back, and when I realized the ceiling was still there, I sighed with relief. *Well well, so that means I actually slept in a spooning position last night. Wow, that is a first.*

Before I could conclude my train of thought, Ninnie was standing by the side of my bed with her hands on her hips like a bad mistress, telling me to wake up and do the dishes because we were going to have visitors today. I was right back in hell. I did not even look at her as I walked past her, dragging my feet on the floor to go take my shower and shake away any stupid paradise thoughts I had lulling around my head from last night. The Diaspora is going to stay at this house after all. I guessed that meant more work for everybody around here who was not going to be busy giving him Australian kisses. *What kind of fresh hell is this? Aie pitié, Jesus.*

I noticed that one of Ninnie's friend was already here fixing her hair, probably for tonight. This one must have married a puppet, because she was here at any hour of the day or night. I imagined it was like being with a person who was constantly on the phone, and one reached a point where it was nerve-racking. I imagined her husband was probably about to enter this last stage, and one of these days something interesting was going to happen to her. It could simply be my wishful thinking, but I certainly wouldn't mind seeing her putting ice on her cheek one of these days. Who was I to judge her, anyway? But it was so easy to slip into the judge's robe and crucify her for her misdemeanor.

I got to the kitchen, and when I noticed all the greasy plates and dirty glasses on the sink, my shoulders dropped. I felt like using them for a throw down and crashing them one by one on the wall around the house before running away. That was an idea I had been cherishing for a long time: running away. I decided I was going to bring my radio, plug it in at the kitchen outlet, and put on some loud music to help me get through this nastiness. I put on an old CD with some Zouk music and turned the volume so loud I couldn't hear the water from the faucet. Ninnie came running in the kitchen and mouthing words that I couldn't hear. I imagined she was telling me to turn off the radio, and then she walked over and tried to figure out how to do so herself. I walked up to her with my hands still covered in the bubbles of the detergent soap, and I told her I would turn it off when I was done with the dishes. She replied, "As long as you wash them, I don't care—just be quick because the music is too loud." After she left the kitchen I turned it up to the highest volume and started laughing at my own rebellion. I eventually turned it down a bit and finished my chore.

Later, after I took my shower, I decided to catch up on some reading and locked myself in the bedroom all day. This was the boring part of vacation, because now I had no obligations and no homework due the next day.

Later in the evening, I heard a deep voice with a faltering English accent in the living room. He sounded like one of those Diaspora who put "just," "so," and "because" in between every word so that people would think they were from the United States and spoke English. I never fell for their tales. They came to the country wearing ridiculous gold jewelry, driving rented cars, and pulling US dollars from their pockets as if they knew we used the same currency around here. They walked into small restaurants and ordered a ridiculous amount of food just to make an impression. I was curious to see what he looked like, but I did not want him to see me, and I didn't want to come across one of those perverts who felt comfortable courting a girl regardless of age. The last one that was here gave me fifty dollars to go buy candy, and he winked at me while licking his lips. Fifty US dollars was equivalent to more than four thousand gourdes, and he gave it to me to buy candy! I felt a bit guilty for taking the money, but that was the last time he saw me. Every time I knew he was coming to the house, I would leave to go anywhere else. He asked for me over and over, but really what did this ugly bastard think was going to happen after he gave me the money? I did not ask him, and I would not feel guilty by thinking that I should do something for him in return. That was their move: they'd prey on the guilt of women after they gave them money; they almost never ask directly. A few of my classmates fell for these traps, and I've heard too many stories of unwanted pregnancies, surprising STDs, rejecting fathers, and school dropouts because of a few US dollars.

I opened my door and couldn't resist the urge to see what kind of face this one had, but at the same moment I heard a familiar voice asking for me at the door. When I heard his voice, I quickly walked to the door, ignoring each and every sinner sitting in the living room. Before my cousin could loudly call my name, I was already at the door, acting surprised to see Sebastian standing in front of my house.

He said, "I have been standing outside for half an hour asking myself whether I should knock and ask for you, but I finally decided why not? The worst that could happen is a crush of my ego when the door closes back on my nose."

In my mind I knew he decided to ask when he saw the gold Satan coming from his Jeep and walk in my house, with Ninnie welcoming him and showing all of her teeth.

"Oh, well, I see you're still alive," I replied, trying to keep my cool so that I wouldn't appear too excited to see him. I then realized his eyes were honey brown, and the street lamps reflecting on his face made them pierce my soul. I got lost in his lips and the caramel color on his neck. His shoulders were strongly under that V-neck T-shirt, and through the thin piece of clothing floating over his body I could imagine the six-pack complementing his posture. *Ca alors!*

"Dara, is that a no?" he said.

I had not even realized he was still talking because I was lost painting my own piece of Picasso. I realized he'd asked me a question—twice."W-what?"

"I asked you if you wouldn't mind taking a walk with me, because your neighbors are about to start a drinking charade, and I'm not sure if you want to invite me in your house."

"Oh no, a walk is fine," I quickly answered, trying to avoid any collision with Ninnie and her friends in the house. "Keep in mind, though, if you're a secret sociopath or predator, I will snap your neck before you even touch me."

"Wow, some warning, young lady! Black belt or what? If you don't mind telling me who I am dealing with."

"Well, that's my secret. I don't talk about my training."

He replied, "Okey dokey. I will make sure I behave, ma belle."

"Oh, don't call me that, please." The image of Joe in his disgusting bedroom addressing me while I was on my balcony came to mind, and I did not want to be thinking about him at this moment.

"Okay. Is there anything else I should be aware of before we leave?"

"No." I smiled when I realized I'd already started to freak him out.

I pushed open the door and asked him where we were going. He replied, "Wherever you feel more comfortable." We both laughed. I decided we would go back to the beach because there were always a lot of people walking around, and I also figured if anything should happen, I would be able to help myself with the casual rock lying around. *How could I even think such a thing of him? Man, my mind is really twisted. Oh well, I have been there and one can never be too careful.*

He said, "You do realize it is just a walk. Why am I under the impression your mind is going a thousand miles per hour? Dara?"

"Huh? What?"

Sebastian stood in front of me with his two hands on my small shoulders. "I can promise you, you have nothing to fear with me," he said while looking me straight in the eyes.

He almost sounded convincing, and I faked a smile and nodded. I truly wanted to believe him, but I found myself walking toward the beach like I was walking to my own crucifixion. When I heard the waves, my mind started to relax a little, and he looked at me and smiled like he'd noticed the change of mood. We walked on the sand, wetting our feet and never saying a word. Then we sat down on the sand, and he gently pulled my shoulder against his chest, and rubbed his hands up and down my other arm, and kissed my hair.

"Do you always kiss girls that way when you just meet them?" I asked.

"Hmm, not that I can remember. You want to know the truth?"

"Of course. I am curious."

"It just comes naturally with you. I feel like you're my blood ... like a sister ..."

Come again? A sister, he said? I took a deep and slow breath, gathered my calm, and put it out there with the least anxiety in my voice. "Hmm, interesting. Like a sister. Who would have thought?" Then he started laughing, and pressed my shoulders against him, and I couldn't help but join him. Then I audaciously asked, "What is so funny?"

He said, "How do you do it?"

"How do I do what?"

"Nothing," he replied. "But seriously, hugging you or kissing you feels natural for me, and I almost can't help it."

That is more like it. Now you're talking. I relaxed my head on his shoulders while admiring the half moon in the sky. "You know, I heard that the sky has no color. It took the color of the sea."

"Oh yeah? Interesting."

"Actually, no, it's the other way around, I think. The sea has no color; it appears blue because of the reflection of the sky."

He asked, "What else you know about the sky?"

"Well, I know the name of a few alpha stars: Mitzar, Polaris, Vega, Orion, Sirius, and Betelgeuse. But don't ask me if I can show you one because I did not pay that much attention in *Pathfinder.*"

He chuckled.

"And I know the name of all the planets, actually," I continued. "The sun, Mercury, Venus, Earth, Mars, Jupiter, Saturn, Uranus, and Neptune."

"Impressive! What are you, a nerd?"

"Nah, it's thanks to Pathfinder. I used to hate it a lot, actually."

"I see." He rubbed my shoulders against him again.

"What about you? What do you know about the sky … or yourself?" I prompted.

"Very slick. I like the way you stick that in there. There is nothing to know about myself, really, except that I am taking this year off to figure out what I really want to study. I do a little bit of everything here and there, helping my parents with their business, but that's all."

"Impressive!" I sat up and tapped his back.

"Very funny," he shot back, and we laughed.

"Well, you do that to me, so I don't see why I wouldn't return the favor."

It was getting late. We sat there for a few more minutes watching the scenery of the waves, the stars shining like diamonds, and the tender light of the moon. Then he walked me back to my house. He pulled me toward him and hugged me so tightly that I thought I was going to be crushed like a bug. We said our good night, and I watched him disappear in the dark—not knowing that we would not be seeing each other again for a long time. I could feel the knot in my heart, but I couldn't know why. He turned around and smiled one last time.

I leaned against the cold brick wall, and my heart sank. I looked at the sky, but there was no answer there, and so I closed my eyes and smelled his cologne on my neck and my shirt. This guy carried the two extremes: he could either be extremely bad so that I couldn't resist staying away, or he was just too good for me. His eyes made me want to push him and savor every last drop from his lips. There is something about him that savaged my whole being. I imagined he would come back in the middle of the night, in deep silence, through the flirtatious wind and whisper words to me like Zeus kept in touch with his son Perseus. And maybe he'd have me float from my bed and join him where the moon cuddled with the sky and where the stars met to kiss good night. And maybe he would bless me with sweet tenderness across the collarbone.

I slowly walked in the house with the most honest smile. For the first time in my life, I walked into this house and nothing seemed to bother me. I saw Ninnie dressed to a T with her hair and makeup overdone, and her friend was hysterically laughing at every stupid joke the Diaspora said, but that did not affect my mood a bit. I had never been so happy. I ignored the pessimistic feeling trying to find a place in my heart to induce sadness, and I waltzed my way to my bedroom. I took my new journal, turned the first page, wrote the date, and let my thoughts organize their rightful place.

There is that love
With the eyes that pierce the soul,
The breath that kisses before the lips.
Undefined beauty,
Heart lifted heavenly,
Not knowing the future,
Careless about the reality.
More like a dream,
Should only last a second—
Minute never does it justice.
It's in the instance magic may sway.

I closed the journal, took a deep breath, and let my back rebound on the bed. I did not understand what was happening, but somehow my body loved it. I looked at myself in the mirror and really explored my posture for the first time. I stood with my shoulders back, and I twisted my neck like the ladies in the seventies. I undressed one shoulder and looked at it as if for the first time. I unbuttoned my shirt and let it slide off my arms to the floor, but when I looked at my breast, I felt like my whole stomach was twisting upside down, and my neck was engorged with blood. For a few minutes I felt like I was suffocating, so I picked up my shirt and covered myself. *Not tonight, not now. God knows when. But not tonight.*

Right after I slid under my blankets, Ninnie knocked at my door—something she rarely did. She sat on my bed, and my heart started speeding again because I could feel the intensity of what she was about to say.

"Dara, I'm sorry, but you won't be able to live here anymore. I was contacted by one of your aunts tonight, and she wants to take you in. She is in town and is picking you up tomorrow morning."

"To go where, exactly—and why? What's going on?" I asked.

"Someone told her a bunch of lies about this house, and God knows if I know who. This person will regret the day he was born. She said she never knew you were here, or else she would have taken you long time ago, so she's picking you up tomorrow. That's all I know. So pack your bags, young lady. I have things to do tonight, so *bon voyage* and good luck."

As if I needed any. Apparently I was like a package going around now. I did not want to start crying or anything, because it was not like I was attached to this house. *There it is, that feeling I had after Sebastian left tonight. I swear I saw that coming. I can never catch a break! Happiness can never last long in my book. I wonder when I will finally find some stability?* I sat on my bed, took a really deep breath, and said to myself, *Well, one more adventure.* I pulled out a big suitcase and started packing my clothes. I took off the shirt still embedded with Sebastian's cologne and folded it in a plastic bag before putting it in my suitcase first.

Around two o'clock when I finally finished packing all my stuff, I took some water from the well and took my last shower in the yard. I lay on my bag to have a last conversation with that ceiling, which has been always a good friend. I tried to be hopeful about that aunt whom I had never met. My hands were under my head, and I crossed my legs and impatiently waited for the sun to rise. *She is probably going to come by early because it sounds like a long trip. Ninnie said bon voyage. I'm sure if I were just going to go somewhere else in this town, she wouldn't say that.* The thought of moving far away triggered some sort of excitement, but at the same time I wanted to keep Sebastian. *I wish I would have the chance to at least leave him a note. But I do not even know where I'm going.*

Chapter 5

My aunt was a curvy lady with a sweet face and a sweet smile. She must have been in her late fifties. She was wearing one of those loose slacks with a pair of orthopedic shoes and a flowery blouse twice her size. Her feet were crossed at the ankle, and her fingers were intertwined and decently resting on her knees as she waited for me in the living room. I caught her scrutinizing everything around her like she knew the changes she would make around here if she were living in the house. When she saw me, she opened her arms, and I went into them as she hugged me tightly. An adult had never hugged me like that. She hugged me almost like Sebastian did last night, but hers felt natural, and I did not have any fear about the agenda of this embrace. She pushed me back to arm's length, and as she smiled tears rolled down her face. That was when she freaked me out a little, because I knew nothing about this lady.

We spent five hours on a bus that took the oddest routes. There were dusty ones, crowded ones, and deserted ones. Finally when I saw the palm trees ahead and the asphalted road, I had the impression we'd arrived at our destination. As we descended the bus, a bunch of merchants ran to us offering us all kind of things to buy. They had bracelets, sunglasses, water bottles, and anything one could possibly need. I saw some local musicians who were barefooted with collars full of multicolor beads, playing their instrument for the passengers who would deposit a few dollars in their hats. After the bus driver handed us our bags, my aunt negotiated a price with a taxi driver, who after a few minutes resentfully accepted to take us. Upon leaving the station, I noticed a big inscription on a wall: a red, blue and white paint saying, "Bienvenue à Jacmel." After a few minutes that felt longer than the five hours on the bus, the driver stopped in a beautiful neighborhood in front of a small house with a front porch and a metal door on the side, which had the number eighty-six written in chalk. I felt instant fresh air as we exited the cab. I was standing behind my aunt while she unlocked the chain that served as a lock to her metal door, and a few girls passing by waved and said, "Hi, Mammie Jeanne." Only then did I realize how silent I had been during the trip. I did not even ask the lady for her name. She asked the girls how they were doing, and they answered in a baby voice that they were fine and told her where they were heading.

I shook my head and chuckled after they explained everything about their schedule for the day. Jeanne turned around, looked at me with her glasses down her nose, and raised her eyebrow. I controlled myself right away, understanding that somehow I'd just done something wrong. After I dragged the bags into the house, she gave me a tour of the house, which turned out to be really spacious. She showed me the kitchen that was separated from the rest of the house, as well as a small house in the yard right before the little garden with tomatoes and all sorts of other plants I'd never seen before. Then we moved in the house and passed by the dining room, which was so neatly fixed with clean tableware precisely distanced from each other, and the tablecloth fit so nice one would think she'd sewn it herself. When I saw the sewing machine in the corner so strongly folded in front of a wooden chair, my thoughts were confirmed. But a random thought came to my mind, and I rolled my eyes and felt so stiff.

She looked at me and said, "And no, hon, I will not be making your clothes." We both laughed. "You and I will get along just fine," she added.

I felt reassured by her words, and I wanted to ask how she'd learned of my existence, but I was not interested in the answer and so kept quiet. "I really love your house."

"My husband passed away last year. It is just me, so I try to keep everything neat and tidy around here. I cannot stand a house upside-down.

I smiled as I recalled how she was observing Ninnie's house when she came to pick me up. When she showed me my bedroom with the queen bed and the built-in closet, she needed not say more. I sat on the bed, and a grin came to my face. I checked through the high window that gave me a view of the sky over the quiet street. "No peeping neighbor," I remarked out loud, forgetting that Aunt Jeanne was still standing behind me. Then I turned around quickly said, "No big bing-bang noises."

She smiled and acted like she'd not even heard what I previously said. "If you need anything, just let me know. We have food in the dining room, so help yourself. Other than that, you can make yourself at home. I am your true aunt, and this is your house from now. Get some rest, and we will talk later."

It was still early evening, and there was no way I was going to get some rest. I unpacked my suitcase and put my clothes in the closet. Then I walked right past her bedroom to the bathroom. The water system was modern—no pulling water out of the well—and there was a door for privacy. The clean towels were neatly folded one on top of the other on a little dark wood shelf, and the shower was inviting and clean. I stepped in and let the water run down my naked body like a big relief.

Only then did I remember everybody I would probably never see again. Of all people, Sebastian was the one name that made my heart sink. I felt a little knot in my stomach when I remembered how kind he was with me, but what I did not understand was that I missed him less than when I first knew I was moving away. I rubbed my neck and closed my eyes under the water. When I caught myself enjoying the moment, I turned the water off, stepped out of the shower, and dried myself.

Jeanne knocked at my bedroom door and gently said, "I have some friends coming over tonight whom I would like you to meet, if you don't mind. I would love it if you ate with us at the table."

"A-all right, sure. I do not mind at all."

A flash of random thoughts rushed through my mind like a sudden rain. *A few friends? What kind of friends? What if she is a madam who picks up young girls and prostitutes them out to rich guys? Her house looks very nice; she must have money, to live like this. I guess I am going to find a way to cope, or maybe I will eventually get so used to selling my body that I won't even mind. Maybe I will get rich and buy a house like hers; then I can move out and change my path. But I would have to leave town because everybody would know who I am. Who is this lady, really? She is probably not even my aunt. I need to start thinking of a new plan because I do not know anybody in town, and I don't even know where I am. People should never be trusted. Though she really looked like a decent person. And I thought my life around predators was over! Now she waits until I finish taking my shower to tell me she has friends coming? For all I know, she could be a psycho. God, I cannot believe I was so naïve and so blind. Really, who would offer to take somebody in her house without asking for anything in return? What was I thinking? That I actually have a family somewhere that cares and wants to do well by me? Okay, I need to calm down and pretend I am all right so that she doesn't suspect I know anything.*

When a cold sweat rolled down my temple, I knew I was really stressed about my suspicions. I took a deep breath, but then I heard a few ladies talking in the house and sighed with relief. *Her friends are females. Thank God! Phew!* I felt so guilty to have had such a harsh judgment of her, but I shrugged my shoulders and decided this was my wall of protection, and it kept me on my toes, so I had to accept this part of me.

I walked to the dining room, and the ladies welcomed me with open arms. Two of them suggested that I meet their daughters, and before I knew it they'd already planned a barbecue to invite the whole neighborhood. *What is this? The prodigal daughter?* Auntie Jeanne noticed the worried look in my eyes, and she replied, "Well, I don't know, ladies. You know I am not too fond of these types of things."

One of her friends said, "Oh please, Jeanne, we'll take care of everything. Don't worry."

"Matter of fact, let's do it on my side of the street," another suggested.

I did not want to be the party crasher, so I said, "That is a very good idea. Besides, I need to visit the town and see how it looks."

"See? I love that kid already," one said, and they all laughed.

The dinner was very informative because the ladies were trying to fill Jeanne in about what had happened while she was gone. Some kids were caught by the river kissing, their parents were warned, and they were forced to end the relationship. Somebody's husband was sick, so the wife wouldn't be able to make it to cuisine class … I discretely retired from the living room, and the ladies moved on to sip on their coffee while sharing all kinds of news from the neighborhood. I decided I was definitely going to visit that river tomorrow morning.

I heard a noise coming from the backyard around six in the morning. I walked to the backyard with my pajamas still on, and I could smell coffee. It was strong, and saliva was already filling my mouth. *I want to drink some of that coffee right now.* I saw a young man in the backyard grinding coffee, and Auntie Jeanne was in the kitchen putting water to boil.

"Good morning," I said.

"Good morning, sweetie. I hope we didn't wake you up. How was your night?"

"It was great. Actually, I love the smell of that coffee."

"Yeah, it came in this morning, and I know everybody's gonna stop by for a cup, so I'm making enough for them all." She smiled while wiping her hands on a white towel by the kitchen door. "Come. I have something I need to tell you." She led me into the house with her hands on my shoulders. "I talked to the director of the university; I know him, and he owes me a favor. He agreed to let you take an entrance test to see if you can attend by September."

"But I am sixteen, and my graduation is not until next year."

"Well, you seem like a bright girl to me. But if you do not feel up to it, by all means, I won't force you. I will register you to the nearest high school so that you can finish."

"Well, will I get a study guide to prepare for the test?"

"Of course you will, my dear," She replied with a certain pride. She tapped my back, rubbed my head, and hummed a strange song on her way back to the kitchen.

I drank the most delicious coffee in the world with my breakfast. Soon I was on my way to my destination, the river. I walked a few blocks and could hear the waterfall, so I followed the sound. I worked my way through a few rebel branches and plants and followed the footprints on the ground. Then I started seeing some flat stone, white grey, and crystal brown, and there it was. The beautiful waterfall kissed the river, and many girls were already bathing bare breasted, with shorts or in panties—there were all levels of undress. They were all jumping in the river and laughing without a care in the world. One of them called me like she'd already heard of me and asked me to join in. I looked around, and she said, "The guys know better than to go on that side of the river. We own this baby in the morning, girl."

I laughed and decided what the hell. I took my T-shirt off and threw it to the ground. One of them helped me undo my bra, and with my hands covering my chest, I jumped in the river between them. The water splashed all over, and they screamed. They ask me for my name, and one of them said, "Dara." She smirked and added, "Sorry, but I think my mom already set our play dates." We laughed at her sarcasm.

That day at the river, my perception of the world changed completely, and that was the beginning of a new life for me. We talked for hours about everything from school to the best places to eat. We left when the sun started to rise high in the sky. We walked, and they showed me around town. Later that day they all came to dine at the house, and I learned this was a usual thing: on Sundays everybody stopped at Auntie Jeanne's house for dessert.

Inhibitions

It is a small garden of delight,
Fantasy that will never see daylight.
Sweet dream of blue sky,
Wonderful goals that could reach high.

Enclosed deep within,
As if the grave needs dream,
A dull mind sings its favorite hymn,
Forever determined to sleep in.

A small step is a little much
Despite its desperate need to be out.
A waking noise is a gentle touch;
Passion is needed for all whereabouts.

Part Two

Chapter 6

Years went by and changed like flowers in season. Three winters ago, Auntie Jeanne had passed away, and that almost served me an excuse to drop out on my last year at the university. I wished she would have fought the impossible and made it one more year to my graduation. She would have been so proud. I missed her every Sunday, and people had stopped coming by because there were no more delicious desserts. I wanted to move on with my life just like every other young girl in town who moved away and migrated to other countries. I wanted to sell the house and get on the road to anywhere. But there was something around here that I could not quite put my finger on, and it drew me closer. I never grew out of my bed, and I decided to turn my auntie's room into a guest room.

I looked at my clock and quietly counted the minutes when my alarm would go off. I felt cheated for being up so early, but when my alarm finally rang, I wished it was still midnight and I was just getting to sleep. The birds started tweeting in the trees in the yard, and in the east the sun was doing its part.

Coffee, shower, grab my keys, and head out. It was a routine I'd developed and learned to love, and working became the next best thing in my life.

"Matt Vancour, age thirty-two, stable condition, no sign of brain injury. Fracture of the radial with possible internal bleeding, but he refuses pain medication," the nurse told me.

I ask, "Another car accident again today?"

"Yeah, motorcycle and a truck. The truck driver is fine and is in the process of being released right now."

"Where is his chart? Any internal bleeding?"

"None life-threatening."

I said, "Okay, thanks. Mr. Vancour, I am Dr. Levine. I understand you were riding a motorcycle. You want to tell me what exactly happened? What do you remember?"

"Dara! Little … My little Dara? Is that really you, girl?"

Half embarrassed and half surprised, I raised my head from the chart to identify the daring man who called me "little Dara." The face looked familiar, but it was near impossible to recognize a face with such a wild, unshaved beard. He had broad shoulders and strong arms, and his height was about six foot two.

"It's me, Doc. I hate to use that name, but they used to called me Mousy back in our old neighborhood," the man said.

"Mousy … ?" Suddenly it was like his face had pointed out the little details about his posture to aid my memory. He had grown so tall and strong. His face came out of the shadows, and I noticed the bulge jutting down his throat and went back to those honey brown eyes that seemed to shine brighter as the years passed. They were eyes I'd fixated on to get many favors.

He scratched his throat and corrected me. "I don't like to be called Mousy anymore. I prefer people calling me by my name, but for you, D, I'll make an exception. I am so happy to see you, girl!"

"Oh my God! I still cannot believe it is you!"

I touched his face and turned it a little, as if he was not real. Then, I realized what I was doing and awkwardly pulled my hands back in my pocket. He chuckled. "And you have not changed a bit, D. Look at you now, all grown up and everything. I am so proud of you! I always knew you would make it. I believed in you, and you delivered big time."

I could not help but laugh because his words were giving away more clues that he was truly the Mousy I'd known ten years ago, back in that repelling neighborhood. Then I quickly shifted my attention to his arm and checked the swelling and his fingers. "Do you feel what I'm doing?" He grimaced, showing how much pain he was in. "All right, we have to take care of your arm right away. Another doctor is going to come take a look at it. I am going to take your number, and if I do not have the chance to see you before you leave today, I will definitely give you a call later."

"Doc, I will take your number that way I can make sure you do not disappear on me like quicksand."

"So much for trusting an old friend, Mous—Matt."

"Well, you were never really fond of me back then. How do I know for sure you will call me later?"

"Come on, do you really believe that? We used to spend a lot of time talking, remember?"

He shot back, "When you needed something from me, of course."

"Was I that bad?"

"Nah. I mean, I always liked you, D, but let's be honest: you did not like frail reporter Mousy."

"You know what? Because I am so happy to see you, I am writing my number down." I placed the little piece of paper in the right pocket of his ruined leather jacket, and then I looked at him one last time, shook my head, and I rubbed his back. "You better call me later."

"Bet my life, Doc."

I turned around and pulled close his curtain. As I was walking away, I heard him shouting, "I am so happy I broke my arm, Doc!"

I thought to myself, *Where did that energy come from?* If anything had changed surely it was his attitude. It was like he was dying and had come back to the living. *Mousy, Mousy, Mousy. My dear reporter ... Damn!* I laughed at my last word, realizing I said it loud. It was like Mousy was already imprinting on me for the few minutes I have seen him. All of a sudden my loneliness was gone; it was like my friends had never left town, and it was like my auntie had never died. Mousy was in town, and Mousy always had my back in the past. But I did not remember ever being happy around him. My thoughts took me back to the days when I used to spend so much time in front of my house listening to him tell me every detail about the gossip in the neighborhood. Somehow he was the only reliable person I knew then.

Whatever it was I asked of him, he would do it, no questions asked. But some memories somehow saddened me—the many times I'd ignored him or yawned in the middle of our conversation, or sent him on his way. He always bounced back. I smiled at that last thought, and all I could sing in my head was, *Mousy is in town.*

The day faded swiftly. I got home early and fixed every misplaced chair and the items in my bedroom. It suddenly dawned on me. *Why in ogres am I fixing my bedroom?* I fought the little voice justifying my unconsciousness with the idea that it was because this was how a young woman was supposed to keep her bedroom. Then I purposely left the faded blue blanket on the bed; that way nobody would be invited in. I waltzed in the shower and looked at myself in the mirror, as I did during my regular routine, but only this time I felt ashamed of my thoughts, so I opted for a pair of jeans and boy shirts instead. The water handled my skin like an endless massage. For a few minutes I stood there, my hand on the wall, reflecting on a broken arm. Somehow I was happy he had broken his arm, too. Then reason started flashing in my head like a bad fire drill. *What was he doing in town? What has become of him? Did he turn into a chimere? Was he part of a secret group of assassins? How did he leave the neighborhood?* But of all my thoughts, there was one I fought so hard to suppress. I turned my back against the wall as the water drizzled on my belly and washed my feet, and memories of that night came back. I remember Junior and his tragic ending, and then I sighed and loudly asked myself, "Matt, did you really kill Junior because of me?"

Something about that last thought made me smile. *A man who will not hesitate to kill for me ...* I could not retrieve in me the guilt or sadness of the situation. I wanted to convince a part of me of the laws in nature, the common-sense law that prevents any man from ending another's life. Part of me believed that in some special circumstances, it was necessary. I could not believe the pleasure my mind had in caressing the thrill I could not control. I also could not believe I never knew this hero's true name. *Matt Vancour—who would have thought?*

Around seven in the evening, the phone rang, and when I heard the voice, sweat ran down my back. "Doc, I'm sorry, but my ride is in the shop, I had to hail a cab, but I just realized I have no idea where you lived."

"Rue Duchamps, number eighty-six. Make a right after the Catholic Church. How's your arm?"

"Useless and painful. Can't wait to be healed because I cannot function without my motorcycle."

"Oh, well, I guess a broken arm is not lesson enough." I was talking to him on the phone like he had always been around and was just calling to check how I was doing.

About ten minutes later I opened the door to a man wearing a T-shirt, faded blue Levis, and dark brown suede shoes—no leather jacket, though. I kissed him on the cheek and smelled his aftershave, which reminded me of how long it'd been since I'd been with a man.

"I spent almost five hours cleaning up for you, D. What was that chingy kiss? Come here, girl." He opened his good arm, inviting me for a hug. I hugged him on his good side and settled there for a minute. "That is more like it."

"Come on, sit down. Tell me, what good news drove you all the way here?"

"Well, I'm here for business. I recently bought land a few miles away from the river. I had this crazy idea for a coffee business, but I don't know."

I sensed the embarrassment in his voice as he told me about his idea. It was that stereotype some of my colleagues had about working and cultivating the land. Some of them thought this kind of job was for people who were not lucky enough to learn to read or attend a good school. So many dying resources were thirsty for valiant hands to start to flourish, but the few *paysans* who embraced that career where the ones who had no other choice to survive—leaving the intellectuals even more room to argue their futile points.

"Wow, that's a wonderful idea! Before my auntie passed away, she used to have this guy who delivered coffee, and they would burn and grind them right outside in the yard, which woke me up every morning. As a matter of fact, I still buy coffee from them, but I don't have time for the whole grinding séance. But I support them a lot, you know."

Matt leaned back on the couch and asked me with a lot of interest if I happened to have some more from my purchase this week. I told him I had coffee for the whole month. I made him some and watched him as he took the first sip.

"Hmm, that is even better than the one I tasted from St. Marc village! This is definitely worth the energy that I am willing to invest in it."

We sat on the couch as a cool breeze passed through the living room. We talked about everything and nothing. I explained to him my voyage from our town to this house and the people I met, my great Auntie Jeanne, how I got into the university, and the day I became a doctor.

He laughed and gave me his honest opinions about how he never thought the house I used to live in was a good environment. He was always waiting for me to show up at the door so he could talk to me, and that was always the best part of his day. He told me how he'd left town after high school and dropped out from the university after two years in a computer program. He went to the university because there were very few options to choose from, but he felt that he was wasting his parents' money for no reason. He shared with me their disappointment when he decided to leave school and open a barbershop, which turned out to be great, and now he'd sold it and ended up in my town.

We spent hours talking about everybody we both knew, but we never talked about Joe, and I never asked him. I also never touched on the Junior subject with him, and he did not mention it. After a long talk on the couch and us ending up closer to each other, I offered to show him around town. He touched my face with the back of his finger, and when I felt my skin shiver, I looked at my watch.

He said, "I know it's late. I'm going to leave in a few."

"I did not say anything," I replied with a smirk.

He said, "D, I remember you more than you think."

"Since when did you start calling me D?"

"I don't know—it just flowed naturally when I saw you at the hospital."

He stood up, held my hand, and gently helped me stand beside him. He kissed my hair and my forehead, and then he said, "You smell like flowers."

"Is that good or bad?" I asked. He laughed, and then I told him it was the lemon leaves with which I showered. After a lasting hug, I walked him to the door, and we said good-bye.

I pressed my back against the door after shutting it, and I felt so disappointed. When I heard the knock on my back, I startled, and then I heard his voice. "D, are you there?" He did not need to say more. I opened the door and waited for the longest five seconds for him to seize my vulnerable lips. I kissed him again and again. The aftershave and his pheromones turned me into melting *chocolat*. When he pushed me against the wall with his unbroken arm, I thought he was going to choke me, but he held my jaw as if he wanted more than my lips could offer. My mindful alert was going off in my head, but this time my whole being responded as if it knew exactly what was happening. I was planked on the wall, too afraid to touch him anywhere and break something, and he slid his hands past my bosoms and squeezed my waist. "I have been dreaming about kissing you for so long." He recaptured my lips between his again. "I never thought I would still feel the same way …" He sighed and rested his chin on my head, but it felt more like he was softly rubbing his neck against my hair. He slid his hands in my braids and held it there. He pulled my hair back, and my neck was exposed. He kissed my neck, and as I closed my eyes, I felt a weight come off of me. He stepped away, watching me twirl my hair and letting the waves break the sound of silence. He slid his hand down from my shoulder to my wrist and kissed my hands. This time it was a good-bye well meant.

There it was—the reason I had dismissed a few relationships over the years, the reason some men thought I was frigid. I needed the sweet strength that could hold me down and crush my senses without hurting a single hair on my skin.

Chapter 7

For the first time I experienced what it felt like to have an official someone in my life. Over the years I had been a mere spectator to long-lasting relationships. At the same moment, I was thinking of the few guys I'd purposely lost their numbers after a few dates, the ones I scared away when I never wanted to take it further, and the ones I calmly shooed away when they asked me to have sex so that I could prove my love to them. For years I had to listen to the love stories of all of my girlfriends. They set me up with men. They would even tell me all I needed was the sex: "Just try it, and you'll see. "What I never told them though was I *had* tried it, and it had tried me.

Then it dawned on me that Matt would probably get tired of my dance as well and leave me. I never thought there would be a day where I would be afraid to lose someone. In my mind I had hoped that one day I would meet a certain guy who would only want to do foreplay and never ask me to go further. This was just that part of me with which I could never connect. I never understood the pleasure someone could get from having a penis thrust inside her private parts, and then moron saying stupid stuff, like he's in heaven. The simple idea of having a man sweating over me gave me chills, and I decided to think about something else. It was not worth wasting time over what seemed to be set as my destiny. They would all leave me one by one, and I would bear my cross till I was buried. It all came down to the same subject: sex.

The phone rang for the fifth time, and I could not bring myself to answer. It was Matt; he was going to want to talk about last night, and then he would probably come over to kiss me again—and this time touch other places he had no business touching. I raised my head, checked the number, and went back to staring at the ceiling. A half hour later, the same number called again, and at this point I was not sure whether I should start hating him or feel bad for not answering.

Then I heard his voice on my machine. "Um, Dara, it's me, Matt. I figured you're probably out, or sleeping, or simply don't want to talk to me. But please don't forget—you promised to show me around town. I am counting on you, so please call me back."

A cloud rushed over my eyes, and it felt like tears wanted to pour out, but then I left the room, walked to the kitchen, and suddenly decided to cook. I opened the cabinet, pulled almost everything out on the table, and stared at them for a good ten minutes with my hands leaning on the tale. I decided baking was not a bad idea after all. I grabbed a pack of margarine, and after taking the little beige wrapper off, I put it in a bowl, poured some sugar on it, and started to whisk it like there was no tomorrow. The phone rang another time, and I realized the medium wooden spoon would break my arm before the butter melted with the sugar. I looked for an old electric mixer that my auntie usually kept in a box on the last shelf in the cabinet. I pulled a chair and reached for it, praying that it could still do the job. Once it was plugged in, it worked like magic. I grated some lemon zest and added vanilla extract and a little bit of rose water. After a few minutes I poured in some Carnation milk. It was unbelievable how after many years of helping in the kitchen, licking so many spoons and bowls while my auntie was whisking what was usually cake for the whole neighborhood, I could remember every step of the recipe. The only thing was that the measuring cups were nowhere to be found, and I was in no mood to cancel my plan because of that. The smell started to work on my taste buds, and I swirled my finger in the middle of the creamy mix and tasted it a few times. My first thought was to grab a spoon and start eating it like that, but the phone rang again. I poured some flour and whisked some more.

"Oh shoot, there is no more cinnamon powder ..." This little detail really got on my nerves. I felt under pressure, as if I was baking for a church. As my auntie used to say, "I'd rather stay home faking sickness than bring a bad cake for them church people to eat." I laughed when I heard myself repeating her exact words, and then I felt a sense of relief because I was the only person who was going to eat this cake. I checked the grocery bags I never unpacked and picked out three of the oranges I'd bought from the seasonal vendors. I squeezed them, sieved the juice, and added it to the mix. I did one last whisking and poured it in a greasy and floury pan. After I slid it into the stove, I turned on my radio and started cleaning every corner of the living room. When the phone rang again, I disconnected the wire from the wall.

When the cake smell started invading the whole house, I checked it with a knife to make sure it was properly baked. Then I cut a big piece and sat on the table in the dark, eating away my pain. The house had never felt so horrifying, and I had never felt so lonely. I plugged the phone wire back in, but it never rang. After every slice of cake I ate, I checked the phone to see if the red light would start flashing and finally ring. The phone had stopped ringing, and some dark part inside of me found relief that my prediction remained true. When the tears finally ran down my cheeks, I could not understand what I was crying about. I cut another slice of cake, this time a much bigger piece, and ate it in one mouthful.

The three knocks on my door almost choked me to death. After I painfully swallowed the dry cake, I gulped down some water, ran to the door, and opened it with a smile. Some women were standing at my doorsteps asking me if I wanted to sign up for some stupid company. I slammed the door so hard that I checked my windows to make sure they did not break. I dragged my feet back to the kitchen. That was it. Just like that, I'd driven Matt away, too. Now back to reality. Nothing good ever lasted, anyway. I looked at the slice of cake on my plate and the rest in the pan, and I felt pity for myself. It was a shame how I thought fattening myself would make me feel better somehow. I covered the cake and went back to bed.

Three hours later, I did not know what to do with myself. It was probably too late for a walk, but what was the worst that could happen to me on the street at this hour? The worst did not feel all that terrifying, so I changed into a pair of long pants and left the house. As I walked through the serenity of the street, I remembered when I'd first moved to this town. It was so beautiful, and the stars were so bright that I stared at them for a few minutes. Then I remember someone—Sebastian. *I wonder what became of him?* I remember the night where I was showing off my pathfinder's knowledge by telling him about the stars … and the comfort of his arms as he kissed my head. The strange thing was that these souvenirs did not make me feel any special way toward him. Not as I felt last night, when Matt captured every essence of my lips. I kept walking, lost in the stars and smiling at what was once the highlight of my days.

"Hey, cherie, you got something for us?"

A cold sweat ran down my spine when I realized how far away from the house I had wandered. I heard the laughs of more than two drunken men. I stopped and I thought of backtracking, but they started walking faster toward me, laughing and making gestures with their heads. I sighed and realized I was in way over my head. *Not like this, not now. They won't touch me.* I did not want to run from them because I felt such strong disgust for cowards who preyed on women to hide their own weakness. I stepped back closer to the pile of rocks on the side of the street. I decided if I was the prey, I may as well consider them a must-kill target.

I was firm and ready for my fate when a taxicab stopped beside me, and the voice ordered me to get in right now. It was Matt. "What in the world is wrong with you, Dara? I see some things have not changed much."

"What are you talking about?"

For the first time I saw a furious Matt. He was never the kind to yell or show his anger in the past. I used to ask myself whether he ever got angry. It got to a point when I even started to think he was simply a doormat. Now here he was, glaring at me with those eyes and yelling at me, and all I could think of was, *What if Matt is a dragon, and he can spit fire and reduce this little town to ashes?* I couldn't help but laugh at the thought of Matt spitting fire with a broken arm. *He is already tall, and he would probably need a darker tan to give more sense to the fire coming out of his mouth.*

"Oh, you think that is funny? You think that's funny?" He paid the driver when we got in front of my house. He stood in front of the house, and then he asked me, "Are you going to open the door, or what?"

"Hey, calm down, man. I never took you for a dragon, but man oh man. It's starting to feel really hot around here."

The more I laughed, the angrier Matt seemed to get, but I couldn't stop. My mind had a funny way of providing imagination. I opened the door, and he followed me inside, locked the door, and checked it two more times. Then he looked at me and said, "We need to talk. Right now."

"Ooo, please don't burn me, Monsieur le dragon …" I said between laughs.

"Stop it, Dara. Stop it right now!" I startled. He balled his fingers into a strong fist and released them like he wished he had two useful hands to shake the sense out of me. All of a sudden he looked so tall, and I felt like a miniature in front of him. "I know, Dara. I always knew. I knew everything. I knew when you jumped into his car, and I saw you when you came back. I saw you from my terrace when you sat on the floor in your balcony. I knew, Dara."

When I saw tears running down his eyes, I could not believe what I was seeing. I gulped my saliva and raised my head. "I have no idea what you're talking about."

"Honey, you don't have to pretend with me. I *know*."

"Oh yeah? Well, what about Junior? Did you … kill him?" A deep silence filled the room. "Since you seem to know everything, answer *me*. Answer me right now, or get out of my house!"

"Yes, I did. I followed you that night." He pulled a chair from the dining room table and sat down.

"And what?"

"After you left his house, I went in to pretend to ask him something. The truth was I wanted to know what had happened between you two, because you had this look on your face that I had never seen before. I knocked on his door, and I did not even say hi before he started telling me how he had sex with you. All the positions he gave you, and how you kept screaming for him to stop and whatever … Listen, that is not important Dara; that was a long time ago."

"What, you don't think I can't handle it? Tell me what happened that night, Mousy!"

He looked at me, and what appeared earlier as dragon eyes turned into a dying flame of sadness. "I couldn't take it anymore, so I left. Then I told his landlord that Junior was having sex with his wife, and he bragged about it every night when he's drinking with his friends outside. The next thing I knew, Junior was found poisoned."

I slid my back on the wall and sat on the floor. "So I was right."

We sat in the dark like two deadly souls, and tears rolled down my eyes. When he heard the sniff and me gasping for air in between tears, he approached me and put his arm around me. I pushed him away. "Don't you touch me! I left him on the floor and walked to my room. I slammed my door and hid my face in my pillow, and I screamed my lungs out. I cried for all the years I had bottled up my pain. I cried for all the days I was disappointed to wake up, and all the last words I had written before going to sleep with the idea that it would be my last night. I wiped my tears with the back of my hand and went back to the dining room.

I found him sitting on the floor; he had not moved since I'd left. When I stood in front of him, he did not even look at me. He was fixed on the ceiling with his head against the wall. "You do not know, Dara. Every morning I saw you coming out of this house was like an answered prayer for me. Every night I went to bed with the fear that tomorrow I would wake up and learn that you'd committed suicide. I prayed more than I ever prayed in my life for you. I cannot lose you one more time, Dara. You have to stop putting yourself in dangerous situations like that. Every time I warned you about something, you went right ahead and did it and exposed yourself to it. I got to a point where I didn't know what to do. You made me feel hopeless. You were always so pretty, and when I saw how these men looked at you when you passed by, I wanted to kill myself because I was so weak."

"We were kids."

"I was in my twenties, Dara. I am so sorry. I should have stopped you when you got in Joe's car. I should have done something."

I said, "You couldn't possibly know that was going to happen."

"Actually, I felt something was not right. I waited for you to come back for hours, and when I finally saw you and the disgusted look on your face, I just wanted to die."

"It's not your fault. He told me we were just going to go for a ride around the city, and although I felt that it was weird that he would ask me to come with him, I got in his car regardless."

"Dara, you don't have to explain anything," Matt protested.

"No, I want to, Matt. I have kept this thing inside of me for too long. I want to tell someone."

Chapter 8

I had just taken my shower, and I was standing in front of the house when he got into his car and waved hello to me.

"Where are you heading?" I asked.

"I'm going for a ride in the city. You wanna come?"

"Hmm, I don't know. It's probably too late."

"Well, I can come back earlier just for you. That way no one will notice you were out."

Really, I should have known. What kind of adult tells a twelve-year-old that no one will notice she is out by the time they come back? I got in his car. When we drove far away from the house, he stopped the car. I asked him why he stopped there, but he did not answer me. Then he touched my thigh. I thought it was a mistake, so I gently pushed away his hand. He left his seat and leaned closer, wanting to kiss me.

I pushed him back. "What are you doing?" I said. I pulled the doorknob to open the car door, but he locked it. He put his hands on my thigh again, only this time with a firm grip. He lowered my seat and started to lay on me. I started screaming, but he put his hands over my mouth and told me that if I didn't stop, he would hit me with his belt. I started to fight with him as hard as I could, but he kept going further with his hands. He pressed his body against mine so that I would stop moving. It got to a point where I could not breathe anymore. He managed to slide my panties down, and that was when he thrust his finger inside of me.

I kept moving around, trying to slide in the back seat to get him off of me. My whole body was on fire, my head was near exploding, and I wanted his finger out of me. He could not have intercourse because I was moving so much. My sandal came off my foot and hit his windshield. He started moaning, and then he got off me. I scrambled to the backseat screaming and threatening to tell everybody what he did. He told me no one would believe me, and besides, they would ask me what I was doing in his car in the first place. When he said that, I wanted to die. I was crying and was restless in the backseat because I did not know what I was going to do. I threatened to kill myself, and then he replied, "No, you won't do that." He complained about how I had him dirty his car with his own sperm and that he had just washed it. He leaned on the wheel, and after a few minutes he muttered, "I am sorry, Dara. I don't know what happened." He knocked his head on the wheel a couple of times and pretended to cry. I screamed at him to take me home, and he did—dropping me off halfway from the house. That was what Joe did, and this was why I have hated him so damned much. Every day I saw this guy living right across my house, and I felt disgusted. He was just a disgusted animal who deserved to be hanged.

*****

Matt said, "If it makes you feel better, he is very ill. Before I left the neighborhood, he was practically skin and bones and was on a regular soup diet."

"Oh yeah? Well, good for him. Matt, did you …?"

"No, although I wish I had something to do with it. I heard some mother went on a voodoo tour for him because of her daughter, and she had him tied up to a doll and tortured him day and night. I don't know the whole story, but I know he prayed for his death every day."

"Well, well. That's what you get for screwing the wrong daughter."

"No, that's what he gets for hurting the most beautiful woman of my life."

"Bad timing, Matt, bad timing. Not now."

I sighed with relief after I poured my heart out to Matt, sharing details of what I had never explained to anyone. Matt put his arm around me, and this time I rested my head on his shoulder. He was here with me, and he would protect me as always. A bird started chirping as if to confirm my thoughts. The sun was slowly rising, and we were both on the floor, close to each other. He rubbed my shoulder, caressed my face, and kissed my hair. I had never felt so safe with a man.

He said, "We should probably go to sleep now—it's already four o'clock. Don't worry about me, I'll take the couch."

"All right, then."

I stood up and helped him do the same. "I'm okay, D," he said. Then he smirked to the idea of me wanting to pull his arm twice as strong to help him off the floor. When he stood, he put his hand around my shoulder and walked me to my bedroom. I kept walking with him toward my bed. "I have a bed large enough for the both of us, so no one is going to sleep on the couch tonight. Unless you want to sleep in my dead auntie's room."

"Very funny. I'll take my chances with you, D."

"Deal."

He took off his shoes and got in the bed with me with his jeans still on. I smiled. "I won't bite. You do know that, right, Matt?"

He said, "Come on, you need some rest, D."

He slept on his back, and I put my head on his chest. Right before I was about to fall asleep, he rubbed my back and whispered, "I will wait for you, D. I will be there for you as long as you need me to be. Whenever you're ready to cross that bridge, I will walk you through every step."

My heart sank, and I felt it again—that desire that captured my whole being when he kissed me. I could hear his heart pounding in his chest as he told me what my senses received as the most honest statement I'd heard in a long while. I wrapped my feet around his and sat on his pelvis. "Say that again, please."

"I will—" This time I seized his lips, draining their every essence. Afterward he asked, "Are you sure about this?"

"I guess we will find out, won't we?" The long embrace I once long dreaded had never crossed my mind as something that came naturally and painlessly. Far from the aggression that I always fantasized would break my will to say no, this moment had nothing sadistic about it. Every second he took to draw a line over my skin was like something had come off my mind. My burden was slowly fading in the far-away mountain, and at this moment all I could do was smile and completely give up anticipating what would happen in the future. There was nothing stupid about mourning heaven because surely earth had never been so blessed.

When I opened my eyes, the pillow next to me reminded me that I was not dreaming. I sighed, smiled, and welcomed my new self in the world of the blessed women.

But I was alone in the bedroom. "Matt? Matt, are you here?" No answer. I pressed the back of my head into my pillow. *Of course he is gone. I am such a fool. How could I fall for this after holding my ground for so long? How could I be so stupid? He is a man, just another one of those men ... And he is gone.*

"Morning, D. Did you call me? I was talking to your milk lady. She delivered your fresh milk this morning. I tipped her, and she was surprised. Am I not supposed to do that?" Matt stood in front of my bed and handed me a cup of hot coffee. I could not say a word. I was somehow disappointed that for once my prediction had failed me. I sipped my guilt away and smiled, and he winked at me. "Do you like the coffee? I hope it's not too strong."

"I paid her double her price at the end of the week."

"What, the milk lady?"

"Yeah, so basically you just made my life more difficult, because she's going to expect tips when she delivers my milk."

"Oh. Well, I am sorry, honey. I will make it up to you."

He kissed me on the forehead, and I glanced at the clock on the wall and realized I should be working today. He noticed and said, "Oh, don't worry—I called the hospital and said you had a fever last night, so you have plenty of time to rest. Or we can go by the waterfall so that I can watch you swimming like a fish under the water."

I laughed. "Well, that's a creepy alternative."

"The last time I saw you swimming, you were with that fancy boy. He watched your every move, that one."

"Oh, Sebastian? Well then, you are *both* creepy. What happened to him?" I asked.

"Huh? What happened to who?"

"You know who. Sebastian. Where is he now?"

"Oh, fancy boy? Yeah ... he is married with five kids now," Matt said.

"Five kids? Really?"

"Yup. Some men don't waste any time."

"Wow!"

Matt left the room, and in the hallway he said, "If you want, let's go to the river now before the sun rises higher in the sky."

"I'll be ready in a minute. You're getting in the river with me—I don't care if you have a broken arm. I'll push you in the water!"

"What? Are you serious?"

"Nah, I'm just kidding."

He kept looking at me as I joined him on the porch. "Are you ready to go?" He pulled me by the waist and hugged me tightly. "I love you, D."

I ignored his comment. "Let's go, Matt. You've got me in the swimming mood already."

"I love you, D." he repeated.

I wanted to believe the sincerity in his voice, but for some reason I felt like he was moving way too fast for me to adjust. It also dawned on me that I really had no idea of the notion in which he was engaging. *Should I say it back? Would I mean it? Was this one of those white lies that can be used to dry some tears or save an embarrassing situation?*

For some far-fetched reason, I missed the fantasy where some guy— less than a stranger yet a gentle stranger—would swirl me into this dance and shower me with words to which I reserved the right not to answer. I could just stand there or lie around and have him have his way without a care in the world about what I had to say or what he was going to say. Matt was leading me to this path for which most women longed, yet here I was, far away from him.

When I jumped in that river, he sat down with a towel doing exactly what he said he was going to do. I smiled at him a few times as I gently moved through the water, aware that I was being observed closely. He leaned back on a rock and got more comfortable. I flipped on my back, fluttered my feet, and smoothly raised my hand above my head and pushed the water so that I could execute my dance. After a few rounds I stood.

"Can I ask you something stupid?" he said suddenly.

"If it's stupid, why do you want to ask?"

"Just curiosity, you know."

"No, I don't." I chuckled nervously. "But ask away."

"Have you ever … you know, touched a guy the way you … you know, last night?"

"Matt that was not really a sentence. I did not understand a thing."

He blushed. "No, I was just wondering … about what happened, and I was curious."

"Matt, honey, you are not making any sense."

"Don't worry about it." He nervously laughed, and it was the fakest laughter I had ever heard—the kind of laughter that sprung out to hide an unexpected outcome. He shrugged the towel over my shoulder, kissed me on my forehead, and then pulled me against his torso and settled there.

All right, that's it. I have to get rid of this man.

Then he said, "Maybe I'm overthinking this, D, but something tells me you're not gonna give us a chance."

I'm glad you got it, Matt. That is exactly what I'm thinking.

Clouds of guilt surrounded me, and my neck got stiff with shame. He did not deserve any of this. It was more like an inner confession for which I should be damned. I walked with him, my hand around his waist, and plotted a scenario where I could gently say the usual words: "I am sorry, but this is not working. It's over." This was by far the most disgusted I had been with myself. *What did he do?* That was the question I always ignored when it came to good-bye. Some way, somehow, it was always for the greater good.

I said, "What? What made you say something like that?"

"I don't know, D. I may be reading too much into this."

I crossed in front of him and walked backward, my hand pointed at his chest. "Let's make a deal, Matt. How about we take it one day at a time? No worry about tomorrow, you know? No 'What if?' We just enjoy each day we have."

"Sounds good to me." He smiled, and it felt like a weight had been lifted from my shoulders. "Now, if you'll be a good girl, I will make today a very special day for you, young lady."

"Hmm, tempting. One problem with that, though."

"What?"

"I'm not sure I know how to be a good girl. I never went to that school."

He laughed as I went back to his arm and slid my hand around his waist. I innocently caressed his back and rested my head on his shoulder. He said, "I will teach you."

My mind wandered to places at those last words. I needed more than one lesson—and on more than one subject.

Chapter 9

Matt had met with a few planters and had settled his business. The coffee exportation was going great, to the point where he needed to open a new factory and hire a few assistants to look over things. This man walked into my quiet and disturbed life, and he swept me off my feet every chance he got. Who would have thought that a year ago an accident would push me straight into his arms?

I raised my feet up and rested them on the veranda while sipping on my ginger tea. I had been told ginger tea and cool weather didn't match, but frankly I could not find any better place in the house to sit. Matt was supposed to have been here hours ago. He had been acting so strange lately that I could not find words to explain his behavior. Earlier today he showed up to the hospital unexpectedly. I thought perhaps he had gotten into another accident. Ever since he got back on his motorcycle, I would think that he had gotten into another accident every time he called or was late for an appointment.

"Hey what's going on? Are you okay?" I asked him.

"I did not get into an accident," he joked while pulling me toward him for a kiss. "I know you're working a long shift today, so I brought you some coffee for a good start."

"Aw, how nice of you, coming all the way here just to bring me coffee!"

"Well, I have to take care of my lady, right? Listen, do you have any plans for tonight?"

"What do you mean, plans? Like am I going out tonight, or if am I going to be busy?"

"Any plans at all," he said.

"Well, not really, but I wanted to go to that new Creole Café in the village for some nice zook music and some tasso. I heard the band is excellent."

"Do you absolutely have to go tonight?"

I replied, "Not really. Do you have something better in mind?"

"Well, I don't know if it's better, but I'm coming over later."

"Okay, no problem, then. But bring your own food because you know I haven't cooked anything all week."

"As if you ever do!" He kissed me on the mouth before I could come up with a reply, although he was right. Not only did he do my grocery shopping, but he also cooked my dinner whenever he had free time. "Gotta go back to work. I can't wait for later."

At 8:30 PM, I heard the sound of his motorcycle raging through the paved street. There was something about hearing that sound from far away; I almost always knew it was him coming. There was that warm, fuzzy feeling that surrounded me until I heard his voice. I had taken the time to fix my hair and apply a brand-new red nail polish on my nails. When he pulled in front of the house and took off his jacket, I noticed he was wearing a white shirt tucked inside his velvet, well-fitted pants, as well as a nice vest to compliment it all. Of course, his sleeves were pulled midway to his forearm. He almost looked like a complete stranger, dressing so classy just to come to my house. I did not know whether I should get up and hug him or just sit back and enjoy this new, handsome stranger stepping onto my porch.

"Do I get a hug or what?" he asked.

"I don't know, Mister. I'm afraid I might crease your shirt."

"Oh come here." He pulled my hand, hugged me, and lifted me off the floor.

"Matt, put me down, please. You've got to stop holding me like that, or else one day we both will end up on the floor!" My mind was screaming otherwise. I wanted to stay exactly where I was and inhale every scent of his neck. I wanted to be the vampire that sucked him dry but leave him alive, healthy, and still handsome.

He put me down and gently pushed me away. "I love it when you wear these shorts. You really look sexy, my lady."

"Thank you, sir. For a moment I thought I should have worn lace and pearls."

"You look beautiful as always. I have a surprise for you, but it's half an hour away. Do you want to ride with me, or do you prefer driving your car?"

"Ride with you, no doubt," I replied.

"Alrighty, grab your jacket and let's go."

He handed me his helmet, and I hopped behind him and held on as tightly as I could. I rested my head gently on his back as I felt the wind on my body.

He stopped in front of a big portal, and somebody rolled it to the side. He drove on for at least five long minutes and then turned off his engine and parked. "If the future smiles in the right direction, this might be your new home, Mrs. Vancour," he said.

Mrs. Vancour? Was that a stupid joke? I said, "What was that you said?"

There on the green grass, glowing under the reflection of the moon and the amber light coming from the bay window of the house, Matt got on one knee and spoke words that I would never forget for the rest of my life. "Dara Levine, I have loved you from the moment I saw you coming out of that house and wearing the most beautiful smile I could ever imagine. I have loved you and prayed for you before you even knew my name. I yearned for the day I would meet you again and manage to open my mouth—not to share some useless news but to convince you to go out with me. Breaking my arm in that accident was the happiest day of my life. Now please, will you be part of my life for the rest of your life and marry me?"

Did he just ask me to marry him? God, is there a way I could visit the house first? Well, the moon is really too bright tonight. Oh crap, I need to come up with an answer really soon. Do I really, deeply love Matt? Do I love him enough to give him the rest of my life? I mean, I love him—I think so. Well, I feel good being with him. Shouldn't that qualify as love? Oh shoot, I think I'm gonna cry. Maybe crying would be a good way to get out of this ... God, what's wrong with me?

This is the Matt I have loved for 365 days now—well, maybe 299 out of 365. That's enough to say the big yes, isn't it? God, crying could really help me right now ...

As I spent the longest seconds processing Matt's request and controlling my thoughts, the heaviest teardrop fell on my hand. I was not sure whether it was from pain or joy, but all I knew was that tears were flowing out of my eyes like a river, and I could not formulate my answer. I knew deep in my heart what I needed, but was that what I really wanted? It was not fair that I needed to sign off on an unknown future in less than two minutes. Either way, I needed to come up with an answer, and Matt's eyes were the last place I needed to look.

Chapter 10

"Yes, of course I will marry you, Matt."

When he slid the shiny princess cut diamond on my finger, I felt the sky come down and envelop me entirely. I felt like I was floating in a place where the oxygen was too low to survive. He was so happy when he got up and wrapped his arms around me. At that moment I knew that I had made the right decision.

He opened the front door, and I stood there in amazement when I looked around that oversized space with the high oak ceilings and the large bay windows. I looked back at him. "Oh my God, Matt, that is huge!"

"Wait till you see the rest of the house."

He then led me to a room which I already imagine as a leisure room, and when I saw the nicely equipped kitchen with the dark wood cabinets and the stove, I told him, "You know this will mean getting a generator, because electricity is not constant around here."

He replied, "I know," with an air of confidence, like he had already thought of everything.

When I noticed the backyard view from the kitchen window, it took me a while to realize that the reflection of the stars through the moving floor was in fact the major factor I had dreamt of having in my house. Then Matt slowly moved behind me, pulled me by the waist, and whispered in my ear, "Are you ready, my lady, for *la piece de resistance?*"

At this point I realized that screaming would have shown too much excitement. I couldn't be jumping around like a baby who saw candy. I smiled and suffocated the explosion of joy in my heart as I walked out on the brick floor surrounding the pool.

"How exactly did you manage to hide all this from me?" I asked.

"As soon as business started to go well, I bought this land. When I sat with the contractor for the plan, all I thought about was what you would like. I hope I did a fair job."

"You do not build a house without consulting with your wife! what if I did not like it?"

He stood there with his hands in his pocket and a smile so wide that would eventually hurt his cheeks.

I asked, "What are you smiling about?"

"You just called yourself my wife, missy."

"No, I said no such thing."

"Yes, you did." His smile grew.

"Huh. I don't remember."

I knew I heard myself saying something like that, but there was no way I could actually believe I meant the word in all of its significance.

I waltzed past him with my dignity somehow intact; there was no place for vulnerability.

We went around the house and opened another door that led to a short hallway with a shower room and a closet that was across a nice little room—the kind of room one found purpose for after one decorated the whole house.

As I counted the steps of the semi-spiral stairs, I glided my fingers on the smooth mahogany that framed it all, and I couldn't help but think of the many treatments each piece of wood had received probably a few months ago. I thought of the many men leaving their homes early while holding their cups of Akasan their wives had prepared for them, sweating over this piece of art, their only source of income with which to support their families. I imagined one man sweating as the speckle of the wood he was finishing flew in the air, and wiping his forehead with the back of his palm as he perfected his love through the noise of his instrument. I imagined his pride when he noticed the smile on his customer's face and got paid for the work of his own sweat.

"This is all so beautiful, Matt."

On the last step I hesitated to turn right or left. I suddenly felt like a virgin walking to the procession to consummate her marriage. I thought of the bedroom I would have to share with Matt for the rest of my life, and then it all felt too real.

"Are you okay, D? Come on, come and see." He walked past me like a happy child and opened his arms, showing me the bedroom to the left. "And this—I was thinking it would be great for a little version of us. What do you think?"

"The beige carpet has no business in this room, Matt. This one has to go."

"Well, it's your house. You do the décor if you want."

Then he scratched his head as if something bothered him. I knew that sign. He'd done it many times before, along with the two lines on his forehead he was going to try to hide in the next minute with a nervous smile and a sigh. *There it is. He smiles and puts his arm around me, shrugging my shoulder. What is that supposed to mean?* The bathroom in between the two closets seemed to get less attention after this little moment, but everything lightened up when we walked in the master bedroom with enough space to move in two bedroom sets. I walked through the French door leading to the balcony, and the breeze of the faraway mountains with the dance of the trees kissed me hello. For a moment this felt like home. I firmly gripped the veranda and closed my eyes for a few seconds.

"Dara Levine, what are you afraid of? Tell me, D. You can just tell me."

"I am afraid of you, Matt. And everything that comes with you."

"I don't understand, D. what do you mean?"

"I don't know. I cannot explain it to you. If you don't get it, then you just don't."

He sighed "Can we not have any half-talk tonight?"

"What is that supposed to mean?" I asked defensively.

"You know, when you say you don't know, and that if I don't get it, then I just don't."

"No, I do not know what you mean, Matt."

"Okay, never mind."

I got angry. "Don't 'never mind' me." I turned around to look in his eyes. "If you have something to say, then just say it—no need to redirect."

"Baby, calm down. I did not say anything."

"Calm down for what? I am not yelling or taking a tone. That's as calm as I can get." He scratched his head, sighed, smiled, and reached for my shoulder. "Don't you touch me, Matt Vancour! I do not need your pity, or whatever that sigh means."

"What in heaven are you talking about?" I quickly walked off the balcony, as if I needed a new atmosphere for the kind of words he had coming his way. "Dara, wait! Where are you going?"

"I'm walking home," I said simply.

"Okay, now you're not making any sense. It's ten o'clock, and it's not like your house is right across the street. Where do you think you are going?"

"You think I need you to pity me and to shower me with stuff, or whatever you're doing? I was fine before you came here, and I will be fine if you walk out right now. As a matter of fact, here is your stupid ring—I don't need it."

"I cannot believe this!" he said in frustration. He caught the ring as I slammed it into his stomach. My head was hurting, my hands were shaking, and I felt cold sweat all over my skin. "You know, if you wanted to say no anyway, you didn't have to make such a scene out of it. I would survive it as I have, many times before."

I was a bit shocked but shot back, "You'd better not be talking about what I think you are talking about! You do not want to go there, Matt. Believe me, you do not."

"Oh yeah? Well, I do. I want to go there, over, and come back. What's with you pushing me away every time we start getting intimate?"

"Well, I am sorry for your unnourished appetite, Matt. I'm sure you can find a way to accommodate your needs without me."

"God damn it, Dara, I was not just talking about sex. It's everything! Every time we start to shift to a better place, you find a way of messing it all up."

"Then *leave me alone* so I won't mess up anything anymore! You ask for marriage, and you're talking about kids, and you build this huge place—and I don't even know if I really love you ..."

"Oh wow! You don't even know if you love me, Dara? Well then, there it is. I have been fooling myself all this time, enduring your nice temper, thinking that she had a rough life but she'll be fine, doing everything in my power to make you feel safe and restore that trust, and trying to make you happy! And you wait *after* I propose to tell me you don't know if you love me?"

Deep in the darkness of my mind, I did not know if I wanted to say these last few words. I hated myself for making him so miserable, and I could not help but thinking how I'd failed to suppress my demons and should have praised his achievement instead. He did not say another word. He walked right out of the house and disappeared in the darkness of the night. While standing in the middle of this big, empty house by myself, I'd never felt so lonely. I felt humiliated with my own thoughts, and I wanted to die for that.

The house started to rotate with me, and I needed something to soothe the pain. There were no words for it, not even in the medical books. It was not a sharp pain, but it was not mild. It was not the kind of pain that makes one fall to one's knees. But I knew I was dying. I slid my back to the wall and sat on the floor. I needed some answers and maybe an instant solution. Tears were mixing with my sweat, and I could not breathe. My hand went to my forehead as if I was afraid my brain would fall out. I could not do this anymore.

Then I saw him. He was standing over me smiling, and he was touching me with his heavy, cold hand. Then I remember the many eyes that undressed me every single day. I heard the mouth that repeatedly said, "You would never be good enough for anyone. Your life will end before it starts."

"Stop it," I replied to them. "I am a medical doctor, and I am a grown, educated, twenty-nine-year-old woman. My life will be fine. Stop it. Stop, stop, *stop it*." I stood up. I needed something for the pain—I needed it now. I wanted to pull my hair out, and I felt like taking my clothes off and streaking through the street. "Stop it."

I ran into the kitchen and pulled open drawers, looking for something to chase these demons far away from me. Then I noticed Matt's toolbox. My heart sank, my skin shivered, and my head spun like I had drunken several bottles of wine. I said to myself, "I will not write any notes, this is about me. No one can understand my pain, and this is about me. I should have done this long time ago …"

"You think it will be worth it?"

I was startled. I did not hear the door open, and I did not hear the steps in the house. Matt was standing by the door and observing me as I tried to figure out how to open the box to my freedom. I said, "Go away. I don't need you. I never did."

He came closer and closer. I pounded on his chest, pushing him away until I felt too weak and just accepted his arms around me.

He pressed me against his chest and kicked the toolbox away. "Baby, I am here. I will always be." He rocked me over and over and kissed my hair. He looked at my face, which I tried to hide, and stared straight into my eyes. "Baby, I am never going away. I will protect you. I will do anything for you. I love you, D. I mean it." Then he mushed my face against his chest again and sighed. It was a deep, long, sincere one; there was no pity, but there was something else. He walked me upstairs, and in the left room he pulled out a twin mattress and rolled off a few sheets. He said, "Come on, you need to rest."

When I smelled him all over the sheet, I asked, "Have you been sleeping here?"

"Only for a week," he replied. He lied close to me and traced lines on my back, perfecting my special backrub so that I could fall asleep faster. He gave me the backrub that had cured my insomnia months ago.

Through the gentle splash of the trees swinging and the breeze slithering through the windows, I could almost swear I heard myself, or some voice from my dream, muttering, "I love you, too, Matt. I really do."

I felt his kiss on my lips, and he drew me even closer to him and said, "I know you do, babe."

Chapter 11

The rhythm of the tambour, the guitar, and the hand clapping from the amateurs far away in the village vibrated the palm trees and crossed the mountains all the way to my window. I stretched and opened my eyes as I welcomed the fresh air flowing in. My neck felt stiff, but when I saw Matt sound asleep on his back with his arm by my pillow, I knew the reason. I slowly excused myself and opened the French door to the balcony. What I saw was unreal. The trees were swaying in the most picturesque movement, and from over this marvelous tableau I could see the entrance of the village where all the amateur musicians reunited to earn their breakfast gigs. They seemed happy, and a few passengers stopped by, danced to the beats, and dropped a few coins in the box before disappearing.

I breathed in the sweet sun rising before my eyes, and then it hit me. *I don't want this monotone life—waking up every morning and driving to the same hospital, and then come back late in the afternoon to my beautiful demeure. I want something more meaningful than the prestige and rewards of being a regular doctor. I want to make a difference in my country. I want to create something that will last even after I am no more.*

Matt woke up and looked at me. "Why are you up so early, missy?" I turned around and gave him a big kiss. "Oh wow, someone is in a good mood this morning!" I walked past him, and he turned around, looking at me and curious to know what was going on. "What am I missing? Did something happen while I was sleeping, or ...?"

"Oh yes, something big. I had a revelation, Matt. A big one."

"Okay. Should I be worried?"

"You know how when you came, you were telling me about your school? You dropped out, sold your belongings, and moved to this town and started your dream career. You mentioned your parents, the coffee, and stuff. And you met the planters and knew you loved it. You have the business, and …"

"Hold on! First of all, stop walking while you're talking like that. Second, I don't understand a thing from what you just said," he said.

"Okay. You know how you started going to school to be a computer genius, and then you realized it was not what you wanted to do?"

"Well, I never said I was going to be a computer genius, but go on."

"You're missing the point, Matt."

"Okay, okay. But just get to the point, hon."

"Okay, here it is. I don't want to be a doctor anymore."

He was clearly shocked. "What?"

" I am going to resign from my job, rent my aunt's house, and open a primary school and teach children to read. I'll inform them of their culture and include a local vocation in their program—you know, a way to cultivate our own resources. What do you think?"

"So you are telling me you are going to give up seven years of school to become a licensed doctor, and a decent, well-paying job, just so you can teach children how to plant flowers?"

"You are being cynical—you're twisting it the wrong way. You know what? Never mind."

"No, baby, I think your intentions are good. But right now you're not making ... I mean, you need a well-thought-out plan. What I didn't tell you was that it was very hard for me to move here. It was not an easy decision, and so far everything is going well, but it's not as easy as it looks. It is time consuming and very risky because the smallest mistake can set me back to square one. And you know, I don't know about this ... Last night you were looking for sharp objects to do God knows what, and this morning you wake up all hyped about quitting your job as a doctor and starting an agricultural school? What's going on, Dara?"

"I did not say I'd open an agricultural school. Wow! You really don't think I can do this? I supported your idea when you first came here. Why don't you support mine?"

"Yes, you did, babe, and I am grateful for that. But all I'm saying is to give it some time, you know? Give it a month. Think about it and make a plan. Evaluate everything, and then if you still want to quit your job, I will support you 100 percent."

"Well, that sounds fair. Okay, I agree. That's a good idea."

"All right. Now, let's go find something to eat."

"Where? For a moment I thought I was on a deserted exotic island."

"The street market is ten minutes from us, and yes, you're right: we are indeed on an island. I don't know about exotic, but our country is a beautiful island."

"All right, genius, you didn't have to get geographical on me. I get it. Thanks a lot."

The market was noisy and crowded with vendors and customers trying to get as much as possible for their money. With no price tag on anything, merchants had to be very consistent regarding how much they wanted to sell their produce, if they wanted repeat business. The scenario was usually something like this: The customers approached and started looking at the produce like they were too small, too dirty, almost rotten, or anything that could reduce the price they were about to hear. Then with a negative gesture they would ask, "Kombyen ou mande pou sa?"[4] The merchants, hopeful about selling something, would quickly get out of their chairs and state the price, and then the bargaining started. The smarter merchants would ask a very high price, though not *too* high to chase away customers, but it was high enough that after a few minutes with the back-and-forth negotiating, the customers would feel that they got a good bargain, and the merchants got the exact price they wanted. There were a whole lot of theories when it came to waking up early to go grocery shopping on a Sunday morning. There were those merchants who superstitiously believed in what they called "lucky hand." If their luck was with males, they wouldn't sell anything to the first customer if she was a female. They believed this would give them bad luck for the rest of the day, whereas a male first customer would make them prosper with their merchandise. The early risers got the best produce, unless one was a regular, in which case the vendors would always save the best on the side for their biggest customers.

---

4   "How much is that?"

I bought a shopping bag from a little boy probably selling for his mother, who'd been sewing them all night. Then we started looking for what would make a good, healthy meal. Matt proposed to cook dinner while I gathered everything to make breakfast. I bought a few packs of spaghetti and some smoked herring with a few nice red tomatoes and sprinkles of water on them. Onions were usually set by three or four; usually the big one was on top of three small ones to make it more appealing to customers. I picked three big ones in the pile instead of the well-fixed lot, and the merchant looked at me, folded her apron between her thighs, and fixed the rolling onions from the basket. Then she mumbled a few words before raising the price on me for not picking one of the lots she'd set. I paid her and smirked, and she smiled when she realized I understood what was happening. Or maybe she smiled because I did not discuss her price and just handed her the money. She offered me some fresh pepper, but I looked at hers and another merchant next to her and decided not to buy from her. Then she pulled the typical trick: she told me she didn't have enough change to give me. I picked what I needed from the merchant next to her and asked her nicely if she could give my change to the merchant when she had it. After I left, I turned around and saw her handing the change she did not have to the pepper merchant. I had acquired enough skills after all these years of buying my groceries in the street market.

I met Matt at the butchery and found him sitting and talking about the soccer game he'd missed last night with the butcher, who was stopping from time to time with his machete in the air to comment on the game while his customers were running out of patience. When he saw me coming, Matt stood up, and the butcher waved hello to me with his bloody hand. I smiled back.

"So how far along is our dinner coming? At least we're getting the freshest meat," I said.

"You see, that's a good thing, right, honey? I haven't been here for long, and I just needed to get a few more things before we leave."

"Well, meet me at the bakery, then. And please, Matt, we need to go."

"Okay, in and out. I promise."

I left him knowing that I was going to have to wait for him because he seemed to know almost all the merchants in this town. I passed a lady who was waving her skirt and dancing to meringue music from a random truck passing; all the while she was holding a large basket of oranges on her head. "Crazy town," I muttered. I stopped and helped her put the basket down so I could buy a dozen. My bag started to get heavy, so I had no choice but to wait for Matt at the bakery.

After a long line, I bought two baguettes and a few croissants, and then I sat on the closest chair waiting impatiently for Matt. After the longest five minutes he showed up and asked, "Are you ready to go?" I did not answer.

My spaghetti was al dente, and the fresh orange juice was delicious. I sliced the baguette, put it on the table and called Matt several times before he hung up the phone and came in the kitchen. *It must have been some soccer game.*

Matt walked in the kitchen shaking his head with the same attitude he'd had at the butchery.

"Who was playing?" I asked.

"Brazil and Argentina."

"Oh. Who won?"

"Argentina." Then he sadly took the plate I handed him and poured himself some juice. "Well, we have no chairs. Do you want to come sit on the cement block by the pool?"

"We have no choice. I'm sorry about your team, Matt. You could have proposed to me another night, you know."

"I didn't want to wait. Come on, let's eat."

"Well, you have to admit, Brazil had it coming," I teased.

"Ooh! You did not just say that, Dara!"

I started laughing so hard that he joined in. Men in this country took soccer games so seriously that one would think they didn't need anything else to survive. These two teams, Argentina and Brazil, had created great controversy everywhere. On some streets, if one was an Argentina fan, one had better avoid wearing it, or the Brazil fans would get in an uproar. Whenever there were major teams playing like France, Argentina, Brazil, or Holland, the streets were calm and groups were formed in boutiques or any houses with a nice big radio or TV. Then after every miss or goal, one could hear an explosion of voices coming out of nowhere, as if the houses were on fire and people were running for their lives. I knew that once this house was finished, I would have to deal with the fact that even the butcher might be coming in to watch the season with us.

I looked at Matt eating his food; he was deeply focused on his task. *Men really need two things: food and sport. And maybe a wife—one that is not suicidal.* I looked at this man who had loved with no reserve and was willing to offer me everything that a woman could desire. He was handsome, he worked hard, and I felt so comfortable with him. With Matt I never felt like I was missing something or had to step on a higher scale to meet his standards. He was a natural, and he made me feel like I was the most beautiful woman ever. This man would take care of me in health or in sickness, as he had before.

"Matt?" I said.

"Yes, honey?"

"I am sorry about last night. I don't know what got into me. I freaked out. I'm sorry for exploding on you like that, baby."

"Ah. Yeah, you really scared me. It's like I never know where I stand with you. You change your mind in a second, and when I saw you with my toolbox, my mind went crazy."

"But you were so composed when you walked in the room."

"I figured that's what you needed. I wanted to be strong for you, Dara, but you have to let me in. You cannot keep things to yourself and then suddenly burst out at me with real bad timing. You have to let go and allow yourself to be loved and to love. You're beautiful, you're intelligent, and you have so much potential, but you are so angry. It is so painful to see you dragging these memories with you everywhere. I want you to heal. I want you to grow into the amazing woman you really are."

Tears rolled down my cheeks, and I couldn't finish my breakfast. I needed a change, and this change had to start from inside my mind. "I don't want to quit my job anymore."

"Hmm, that was quick. What happened to teaching children how to plant?"

"Don't push it, Matt," I warned. We both laughed.

"Well, it's not me, honey. You are the one who wanted to go knock on parents' door and borrow their children for gardening lessons."

"Nah, it wouldn't be like that. I still want to open a school, though for the less fortunate. Children on the streets everywhere need people like us, you know."

"Now *that's* a good idea! That makes more sense to me than the agricultural school."

"Oh yeah? Are you really going to group yourself with the 'intellectuals' who think this is not important?"

"No, au contraire. I think in order to do something like that, you have to at least have a background so that you can know what you're teaching. You spent almost a decade studying medicine. What makes you think you can just shift to agriculture in one day?"

"Whatever, man. You did it," I pointed out.

"No, I did my research first, and that's why I ended up in this town. And I am so glad I did."

Around noon, Matt decided to start making dinner. "Can I come in the kitchen and watch you cook?" I asked. "I'll be quiet. I'll sit on the table in the corner, and you won't even know I'm here."

"It's hard to imagine you sitting quietly, but of course you are welcome, my lady."

"Okay, let me do a few rounds in the pool, and I'll be right in."

After about an hour, the smell of the fried goat reached me by the pool, so I bounced out of the water, wrapped the towel around my chest, and curiously walked in the kitchen. I saw grated carrots and cabbage with pepper. The pikliz was already done, and the goats were clearly under the stove. Matt was frying plantains, and when he took the cover off one of the pots to add some butter, my mouth watered when I saw the black rice.

"Oh my God, you've really outdone yourself, Matt. You are making my favorite meal!"

"Tasso is both our favorite meal, honey." I walked closer and kissed his shoulder, and he turned around and kissed my lips.

"I have to admit this is all really sexy, Mr. Matt Vancour."

"Anything for you, Mrs. Vancour."

"You know, Matt, I was thinking ..." I took some of the pikliz in my hands and went to sit on the table at the corner. I chuckled a bit and fanned my tongue with my hand. "This is very spicy."

"Too spicy?"

"No no, it's good. I just swallowed it too quickly." I poured some of the orange juice from this morning, and after three big gulps I was good but couldn't help my teary eyes.

"Are you sure you're all right, D?"

"Yes, I'm good. I was thinking, what if we have a destination wedding? You know, elope just the two of us, with a priest on the beach in our chere ville du Cap, and maybe we can even stay there for our honeymoon."

"Well, that's a good idea, but we know so many people from there. I was leaning more toward Saint-Domingue for our honeymoon."

I persisted. "Come on, baby, it'll be fun. We won't spend as much money, and we don't have to go in town. We can stay at Labadie and enjoy the beach, the arts, the sun, the smoke of the fresh fish on the grill … Come on, we can stay there as strangers and drink coconut water and all." I was so excited about the thought of going back to la ville du Cap to visit. I did not have particularly good memories of the people there, but I had always loved my native town.

But Matt was not too thrilled about the idea for some reason. "Well, I'll think about it."

"There is nothing to think about, honey. I have to start making a list of things I need to get to furnish this house, and the sooner we do this, the faster we can move on with our lives. I have to order furniture, move out of my aunt's house, and other stuff. You know we have a lot to do. Right now we both could use a nice vacation. It's like killing two birds with one stone."

"Killing two birds with one stone for our honeymoon? Not very romantic of you," he grumbled.

"Come on, you get it."

"Yes, I do." He sighed. "All right, on one condition."

"Shoot."

"We get married here, and *then* we go to le Cap for our honeymoon only."

"Fine, sir. I'm happy you're on board. Now it's time to start planning it all!"

I jumped off the table and went through Matt's stuff to find a pen and some paper so that I could make a list of what I needed for this house. *I wonder why Matt did not like the idea of going back to le Cap? It's not like we are going to go see everybody we know. Besides, what interest do I have in seeing anybody I knew? I miss absolutely nobody—well, no one I can remember ...*

We sat on the balcony of our empty house with no chairs and enjoyed our tasso. The troubadour from the village added elegance to our dinner as we fixed a bed on the cemented floor. The food was a delight, and we couldn't get enough of the music. At some point we did wonder whether these musicians were ever going to get tired, but eventually when the rhythm started to sound a little off, we knew they were going to give up. We did not want to bother fixing another bed inside, so we slept au claire de lune.

Part Three

Chapter 12

There is something about marrying a man who absolutely adored me. It was like taking a freefall, and in order to do that, I had to close my eyes for an instant and trust that gravity still worked the same. To retreat is to say, "Hey, I am afraid. I know this is great and exciting, but I can't do it." But falling is sometimes questioned by the mind following a multitude of thoughts that demand certain discretion.

The day we arrived at le Cap, my heart was beating so hard that I thought I was going to pass out. Matt looked at me and asked if I was okay. I lied. "Yes, I am. It's just honeymoon jitters," I joked. A friendly staff welcomed us, and the hotel was just as I'd expected: comfortable, a nice view of the beach, and a great breeze—an earthly paradise. I slouched on the bed and let my nerves relax; this was just what I needed.

Matt said, "I am going to go see what they have for us to eat at the restaurant downstairs. I'll be back. Get some rest, D—you look tired."

Why go downstairs to check what they have to eat? What happened to phone service? This thought floated in my mind at the same moment my eyes closed.

I dreamed of a commotion happening outside my window, and I jumped out of my sleep and realized it was dark in the room. When I approached the window, I could still hear the voices of two people arguing; it was all too real. This wasn't a dream. I looked through the shutters and saw the silhouette of a woman and the back of a man that I knew. Of course I knew him—I'd married him yesterday.

I was curious. Why would Matt leave me here in this room by myself to go argue with a woman who clearly knew him? I grabbed his shirt that was on the bed, wrapped it around me, and went outside with the intention of introducing myself. As I got closer, Matt lowered his voice and muttered something to the woman, who suddenly caved in silence.

"Matt, what is going on? How long was I sleeping, honey?" I wrapped my hands around him and raised my head, waiting for his kiss. He gave me the most sincere kiss, the kind of kiss one gave when one feared there would not be another chance. Then I caressed his back and smiled. "Are you going to introduce me to your friend?"

"You married Dara?" the woman said.

Why does everyone seem to recognize me before I can put a name to the face? Matt did not even have time to breathe before answering me. I turned and took a long look at the woman, who was wearing low-rise jeans with just a sport bra. Until she'd mentioned my name, I'd barely noticed my new husband was having a conversation in the dark with a woman who was half naked. Maybe I was just jealous of her 36C size, but I fixed my posture, raised my chin, breathed in to close my chatterbox that was about to go off, and smiled. "Do we know each other?"

"Do we know each other? You must be kidding me, Dara. So this is what happens when you become a doctor? You can't recognize an old girlfriend?"

"I am sorry, but this is not helping."

The woman pulled my hand and dragged me to the light. As I followed her, I almost worried that I may have to pull my hand back from her. Then I recognized the sixth little finger. Of all the friends I had, only one was stubborn enough to pull me with such daring, and only one had a sixth finger; we used to say that was because she'd eaten her twin sister before being born. I stopped, happy and confused about the revelation and the current situation. I hugged her, and she almost lifted me up with her embrace.

"Jessica! My god, you are still here. What have you been up to?" I asked.

"Glad to see you came to your senses. I was already planning on kidnapping you and banging you in the head for days until you remembered my name."

"You have not changed one bit—always bite off more than you can chew."

"That you are right! And I bet you this time I learned my lesson." She glared at Matt. I looked at the two of them and hesitated to ask the obvious question. Matt was standing and scratching his head, almost restless about the situation.

"All right, ladies. When you finish reminiscing, Dara, you know where to find me."

Jessica shook her head and said, "Men. You really think you're getting out if this one, huh?" She was practically begging me to ask the question, but I was not sure I wanted to know, and I also felt like

I needed to give Matt a chance to explain himself without having to interrogate him on a subject that was far overdue.

After Matt left us, Jessica patted my shoulder. "Maybe one of these days we can even agree to get in bed together, or even have une ménage à trois."

"Jesus Christ, Jessica! A little respect, please. Dear god, what has growing up changed in you? Nothing at all."

"Oh please, Dara, do not wave your purity flag at me. I see growing up has not changed you, either. You're just sweet, dear Dara who's never too involved but always gets the hot guys. Speaking of hot guys, what happened to you and Sebastian? Never would it cross my mind that you would marry Mousy."

"Don't call him that. He is a very good guy. Just because you've met his testicles doesn't automatically qualify him as a bad guy," I shot back.

"Finally some straight talk out of those luscious lips! Seriously, I always envied your lips; they are so violet, so nice."

"Should I stay away from you?"

Our laughter echoed on the beach as we spent a few minutes catching up. She told me about her life—and her daughter.

"I cannot believe you have a baby daughter, Jessica! I would love to meet her."

"Yeah, she's my pride and joy. And don't worry, Matt is not the father. Your husband left town without even breaking up with me first. I am sorry, Dara, but he is a coward."

I ignored her jab. "Well, I am so happy for your life. You sound like everything is working out fine for you. A daughter, your own place, and a great job at the airport. That's more than most women can afford in this country.

"Yeah, I thank God for that."

Frankly, I did not want Jessica to tell me about what happened to her relationship with Matt, and I did not want to give her the vibe that we were going to be best friends. As for Matt, I stayed on the beach a little longer on purpose; he deserved the anxiety for omitting this huge detail. Jessica and I really had nothing to say; we did not know each other for that long when we were young, and what I remember the most was that she always had a boy she wanted me to meet, but that was all. She offered to go to lunch before I left, but I was not interested. The fact that she dated Matt really did not help, either.

"Oh, you know Sebastian is in town every weekend. The next time I see him, I'll let him know you're here," she said. Before I could open my mouth to say anything, she kissed me on the cheek and said she had to go because her ride was leaving.

Why would she even mention that last detail when she clearly knows I am on my honeymoon and am happily married to Matt? Jessica was always up to something and I did not trust her a bit. I never really had.

She was always funny, and I loved to laugh with her, but for some reason we never really clicked.

On my walk back to the hotel, I thought about seeing Sebastian again, and the idea did not bring up any guilt. *I should have listened to Matt about not coming here. We will leave tomorrow to our next destination. Le Cap is getting too treacherous.*

I took my time, slowly dragging my feet in the sand, and with each step I turned around to admire the beauty I had missed after being so far away. I could see Matt standing behind the shutters of our room, and the amber light behind him intensified his posture. For a moment I wanted to forget anything had ever happened. I wanted to shoo away that he was ever with Jessica, but something inside of me was restless. Matt was not the kind of guy to follow every skirt flirting his way. I remember one night he revealed to me that he never got involved with any girl he didn't feel comfortable kissing. Kissing— here was something I did not want to imagine happening between him and Jessica. It was one thing to put someone on a pedestal and quite another to discover he was just a man after all.

When I finally reached the jalousie door, I swung it open and let it clatter back against its frame. I found him sitting on the bed waiting for me.

"Dara, babe, I thought you were never coming back. Jessica and I were nothing serious. She had other boyfriends at the same time she was with me. When you left town, I was really, deeply lost."

"Well, not lost enough, obviously, because you had the time to conceive a daughter."

"I just learned about her tonight, honey. I am really sorry. I did not know Jessica was pregnant when I left, and I certainly did not leave for that reason."

"What do you mean, you did not know until tonight?" I moved across the room to the darkest corner and stood there facing the wall. I creased his shirt tighter than anything I'd ever held and closed my eyes to suppress any energy I might risk losing.

"I met Jessica downstairs, and we started talking. I told her I was married, and then she announced to me that I had a daughter. Dara, please, you have to understand this was before I'd ever met you! I know you and Jessica were friends, but it was never something serious. I love you, and I have always loved you. She knows that, and—"

"Matt, stop." I turned around and put my hand on his chest. "I should apologize. I should have listened to you about coming here for our honeymoon. The truth is ..." I felt like the worst married woman. The truth had been on my lips for some days, but there was really no good way to articulate the words that struck. I looked at his eyes, and I could believe every word coming out of those lips that comforted me at so many occasions, but I could not believe the thoughts from my own wandering mind.

"The truth is what, Dara?" he asked.

"Could you not raise your voice at me?"

"I cannot believe this," he muttered. He sat on the bed with his shoulders bent, and his eyes pierced right through my soul. "I have never felt so stupid in my life." Then he rested his head on his hand.

"Dara, you played me inside out. You twisted my mind and changed yours whenever you felt like it. It must have been some childhood romance between you and that Sebastian."

"I did not say I came here for him!" I protested.

"Then tell me why you would want to come back to this town, if it's not for that? That fancy boy of yours. You accepted my ring and said vows to me. Does that mean anything to you? Do I mean anything at all in your life? From the day you realized you felt something for me, all you've been trying to do is set us up for failure. With you, I can never know what tomorrow is going to bring. I know you feel the same way about me. But you know something? Fine. May I please have my ring back? This relationship was over before it started, anyway."

"Matt, I am not giving you any ring back. It is not what you think! It's just that—"

"Just what? Say it, Dara! Yeah the love of your life. How long did you know that guy back then? One week. One week, and you fell in love with him, and I have been with you almost all my life. Keep the ring if you want, but I'm gone."

"What about your daughter? Why did Jessica tell me she's not yours? Did you tell her not to say anything?

"You and I both know if I was the father, Jessica would have tracked me down already. She knows exactly who her baby's father is, and it is not me."

When Matt grabbed his bag and flung the door open, I stood in one place, petrified that I was making a huge mistake—but for some reason somewhere in a dark corner in my heart, I felt a thrill I hadn't felt for a long time. It was a thrill I was so used to embracing every night before I slept, a thrill that induced so many rivers of tears that I started to enjoy the wet, cold path they drew from my cheeks to the middle of my breasts. When Matt left me that night, I felt the familiar sadness and closed my eyes for a few moments. I was confusingly relieved.

To all the birds and the breeze that may carry this message, let them know I tried. I crawled into the shells and wrapped myself with thorns. I stayed far away, locked my heart, and misplaced the key. Was it on purpose?

I had it all planned: endless fantasies to rock me to sleep, a beige wall to keep me stable, no colors to awake the senses, enough routines to bury me when the time comes. The time I wished too soon. I hate the reality. I don't want the facts—they are overrated. Let me daydream and cry, and hurt and cry, and talk to my ceiling. He just wouldn't go. He just wouldn't go. This change in me, this life, this fresh air he brings around that closes my eyes and invites me to fall back with no worries—it's just too good. I do not want it.

To all the birds, this is what I am feeling. He is gone. He did not stay. He did not ask; he is gone. So gone that I am now lethargic. So gone that my demons came back to make love to me last night. So gone that my sadness put a smirk on my face. He is finally out of the door. Man: a creature I haven't quite gotten the use for, yet he makes such an impact on my path.

Dear diary, it has been a long time, but I am back ...

Chapter 13

It was never enough. I could not love someone with such a cold heart. Never in my life had I met a woman with such contempt for my kind. It was painful walking away from her, but it was necessary. I did not need this.

I left Dara standing in that room with no compassion on her face. She had no remorse, no sympathy, nothing that could be read in her words or on her face. She was just empty—but filled with hatred. I thought about selling the house I had built for her and moving to a small apartment, but I wavered. Was it because somehow I thought she might one day come back with a smile and move in with me? How could I fall out of love with someone I had loved all my life?

When my phone rang for the third time, I decided to pull the wire out of the outlet. If that was her, I did not want to hear about it. This woman had wrecked my soul. I hated her for not loving me back, and I wished I had never moved here.

Several hours later, I was wondering about everything she could be doing and thinking that maybe by now she was already with that Sebastian, reconnecting and talking about whatnot. She would lure him into her embrace, and then they'd kiss, and he would touch those lips that would probably never pronounce a sincere, loving word. He would slide his small, probably feminine hand toward her beautiful neck, and she would smile and close her eyes. I wanted to close my eyes and rest, but I kept seeing her face in a soft dance and her daring eyes between the lights of a few candles. I could not for the life of me believe that some other man was in my bed on my honeymoon. I plugged my phone back with some empty hope that she might call again, even if it was simply to confirm what was on my mind and to say, "I never loved you." The phone never rang. She was responsible for this mess. She was the twisted one with an empty heart and beautiful, cold lips. *Damn you, Dara!* I hit my fist on the cemented wall and focused on the pain cutting my fingers. *I will not call her back,* I said to myself. *She does not deserve my sympathy.*

After a few weeks of mourning the devil that would forever haunt me, I decided to go out and settle the score. If my ex-wife could have empty sex, then why couldn't I?

Weeks turned into months, and before I knew it, 2010 was already here. On a cool morning in January, I woke up with a terrible headache. I called the factory and let my assistant know that I would be coming later in the afternoon.

"Frank, how are you?" I said.

"Hi, boss. I am fine. The delivery already came this morning, and I took care of the inventory. I will be proceeding with the packaging tomorrow, and everything should be shipped by Friday."

"Frank, it's all right. I am not calling about the job. Why don't you guys take the day off today?"

"Are you all right, boss? Would you like me to call down at the restaurant to bring you something?"

"Not today, Frank. I am fine. You can close up for today. Take a nice day off to enjoy with your family. I will not be coming to work today, anyway."

"I am sorry to hear that. If there is anything I can do to help, please let me know."

"No problem, Frank. Thank you. I will see you tomorrow."

I hung up the phone and stayed in bed, lying like a dead animal and thinking about what I was going to do with an empty calendar. For some stubborn reason, something in me felt like I deserved that headache, so I did not look for a remedy. I walked through the empty rooms upstairs and decided I really needed to rent this house. When I opened the door to the master room, it smelled rusty and old. I hadn't been in there since the night before I went to le Cap. I stood in front of the door, and Dara came to my mind. I opened the French door to the balcony and remembered how much she enjoyed standing there. I wondered whether it was time to settle this once and for all.

I went back downstairs to the little guest room I had been occupying, and I looked through an old address book to confirm and dialed the number. Each ring was like a strike to an old wound, and when I heard the familiar voice, it was like a relief.

"Hi, you have reached Dr. Levine. Sorry I missed your call. Leave your name and your phone number, and I will get back to you as soon as possible."

"Dr. Levine"? Dara never refer to herself as a doctor.

126

If there was one thing we used to argue about, it was the fact that she was a doctor who barely worked. I redialed the number and got same voicemail, so I decided to call Jessica.

"Hello, stranger, what's up?" she said.

"Hi, Jessica. How are you? Listen, do you have any news about your friend?"

"Oh! Quelle est cette histoire![5] I thought she is your wife."

"I know she was supposed to be there for a meeting today. I cannot reach her and don't know if everything is fine."

"Of course. Why would I think you called to ask how I was doing? Anyway, your wife is not in town yet, I would have heard because she is a big-shot doctor."

"What do you mean?" I asked.

"She worked at the general hospital in the city for a few months after you left, until she decided to become Mother Theresa and move to Port-au-Prince. And please, Matt, stop with your game. I know you guys broke up."

"Well, she had other plans, and I was not the right one for her, obviously."

"This is what I hate about you men. If it was you trying to get your act together and work hard in your career, she would have supported you. But you stupid men just love to give women ultimatum between

---

[5] What story is this?

you and their career. But anyway, I'm not sticking my nose to your business, because Dara never told me anything. But it was obvious."

"Well, it's hard to agree with you when we are thinking about two different subjects."

"Yeah, yeah, whatever. Your smart ex is out there saving the world, mon ami. No one can reach this woman, and when you do, it's always a five-minute rushed conversation. If you can't reach her through her cell, there is nothing I can do. Or maybe she saw your number and just doesn't want to talk to you. I would have done the same thing. All you do is run, Matt. Remember us."

"How's your daughter by the way?"

Jessica said, "Oh, I sent her to her father for the week. She's better than I am. I am getting ready for work, man. I will call you later. Good luck with smarty pants. Tell her I say hi, and tell her Sebastian was a good catch, and he still asks about her—very often.

"You tell her yourself, and tell your Sebastian that she is taken and has been for a long time."

"Yeah, right. Please. None of you ever stood a chance with Dara."

I hung up on her last words. I did not have time to waste with Jessica. If there was one thing this girl was good at, it was gossiping about people's business.

I decided to call later in the evening with the assumption Dara would be more available. Three hours later, my phone rang.

"Hey, Matt, it's Dara."

My heart was beating so fast that I forgot everything I had planned to tell her. Her voice had the power of a tiger. I was subdued and forgot why I'd resented her for so long.

"Are you going to talk to me? I can hear you breathing, Matt. Besides, you called me. Anyway, I am happy to hear from you. It's nice to know you're alive."

"Y-yes, I am indeed alive," I managed.

"What do you say we talk later, around eight o'clock? I have a few more patients to see today. I will call you later, okay?"

"No, I will call you."

I could see her smile. This woman's smile used to turn my day around. I could feel her warmth, and I completely forgot that she was once bitter. All I could remember was how happy I was with her.

"Alrighty. It is really nice to talk to you. You don't know how much I hate myself for this."

"It's okay, D."

"And Matt, if I ever forget to say this later … It was never about Sebastian. It was never about not loving you. I was deeply lost and might have mishandled a few things. But you and I … you know it was something."

"Yeah. Something," I mumbled.

"Okey dokey. I will call—I mean, I will be waiting for your call later."

"Okay, D. I am happy you are doing fine."

I heard a few noises in the background like she had just stepped out of a room, and I heard a woman saying, "Dr. Levine, Mrs. Johnson asked to see you privately. She has bruises on her lips again—she said she fell." Then I heard the click, and she was gone. But I was hopeful about what may happen in the instant future.

Around six, I stepped out on the balcony and stretched. I realized my headache was gone. Suddenly I felt the house shaking with me, and it stopped. I could not understand what had just happened. Then I heard people from the village screaming, "Oh mon Dieu! Au secours!" Then I heard a guy screaming, "Port-au-Prince, nan cho!" My heart stopped. What I felt was an earthquake.

I ran downstairs and got my motorcycle. Even if the world was falling apart, I was going to Port-au-Prince today. I stopped for gas and ran into the butcher. He took my key. "Matt, I am sorry, but I cannot let you ride a motorcycle to Port-au-Prince. That is insane."

"You'd better step back, man. I am not staying here and to do nothing. I have to go get her. She needs me!"

"Matt, I am sorry, but it is a mess over there right now. You know what? Let's take my truck. What do you say?"

I kept redialing her number, and it kept going straight to voicemail. I became compulsive and could not stop. I felt so stupid. I did not talk to her this morning to let her know how much I missed her and loved her, and to tell her I was sorry.

The butcher came back with his keys and a look on his face, and I knew it was the end of me. The earthquake was nothing compared to the rush inside me.

"Matt I don't think it is a good idea to go now."

"Just shut up. Shut up! You don't know what you are saying."

"Matt, Port-au-Prince is rubble."

"Well then, I will bury her corpse myself. I am going over there."

Never in my life had I seen such a disaster. People were lost in the streets and still terrified about what had happened. Midway I caught a ride with the first aid ambulance; I lied and said that I was a doctor. I stepped out in the mad crowd, watching my feet so that I didn't step on bodies, and looking for a place for which I had no address. I asked a few paramedics on the scenes who never even looked at me because they were busy rushing through the streets and helping whomever they could. I was being pushed and shoved; a few guys had already stripped me of my wallet. I was walking on the streets deaf, looking for her in the mass of white coats. Tears ran down my eyes like hot blood. I was sweating and could barely see where I was heading.

"Over here! I need help!"

My heart froze. I turned around and saw a woman wearing faded, dusty jeans with a shredded T-shirt, and her coat was missing half of a sleeve. I recognized her dark, rebellious hair, which was half in a ponytail.

"Over here!"

She was standing on top of a rubble pile and holding the arm of a woman, trying to help her come out of the hole she was in. I rushed and started digging, pushing aside every block of the broken wall, and we helped the woman get her head out.

"Matt? Oh thank God! Matt, you're here! I can't believe this. Are you all right? Are you hurt?"

After one last pull we got the woman out, and she got up and ran into the street, traumatized.

"Yes, I am," I said. "I am here. I'm okay now. We'll be fine, honey."

"I just … I just stepped out. I wanted to talk to someone. You know, I don't know what … what happened. The building just collapsed right behind me. I … I don't know what happened, Matt. Oh my, I am bleeding."

I saw the blood rushing through the fabric of her jeans. "Come on. We need to take care of your leg."

"But these people, Matt. We can't just leave!"

"You won't be able to help if this leg gets infected. Come on."

She stood there in one spot, and I could see that she was in shock. She was looking at me with those beautiful eyes drowning in her tears, and she could not move. I lifted her up and realized she had lost a few pounds. I kissed her forehead and walked to the nearest ambulance. This time I was not going to let go of her no matter what. She was my stubborn woman, my mysterious wife, and she always would be.

She held my neck and touched my unshaved and sweaty face like she just remembered who I was. "I love you, Matt."

"I love you, too, D. Always."

Part Four

Chapter 14

Worse than being alone was being with a man who hated himself for loving you. I saw it on his face and in his eyes. When he said, "I love you," he wanted to cry instead of smiling at me. I felt trapped. I couldn't leave because he would not let me. I felt terrible about every single bad thing I'd done to him. I purposely pulled the sheet from him at night and left him shivering in the night, and the next day I wanted to kill myself for doing that to a man who loved me. Spending nights with strangers seemed more appealing—at least they didn't know me inside out.

Matt had not talked to me for weeks. I mean *really* talk, not just "Good morning, babe. Did you eat, D? Do you want me to bring you anything after work?" I meant sitting down with him and talking for hours while he drew his fingers on my skin and kissed my hair. I meant sitting on the balcony together and listening to the troubadour from the village, or sharing and laughing about the nonsense that popped in our heads. I meant waking me up in the middle of the night when he came home from watching football over the butcher's house, and wanting to explain to me what a wonderful match it was. He didn't touch me for more than five seconds, and what killed me was when he said, "Oh, I'm sorry," as if to say he didn't mean to do that.

The truth was, last week I told Matt that while I was in Port-au-Prince, Sebastian came to see me. That's all I needed to say before he cut me off. "I don't want to know." What came over me to tell him only weeks after getting back together? Somewhere inside of me felt like I owed him an explanation about what I did while I was away. I felt guilty for keeping the fact that I saw Sebastian while I was away, so I wanted to come clean. We had a "no secret" type of relationship; he knew everything I had done, what had happened from the day I was born till I became an adult. For some reason I felt he deserved to know that one little detail, but I was wrong—big time. Didn't I know he was with more than two women while I was away? Of course I knew. The list included his beautiful brand new assistant, who was of course still working with him. But now it was like seeing Sebastian for a week took away the purity in me and vilified my skin, and he was so cautious not to touch me. It was one more thing to use in our hurtful, slandering argument.

He would never know—at least not for now—that Sebastian never saw that birthmark on my upper thigh. Knowing Matt, he was probably imagining the worst-case scenario, where Sebastian and I went all-in with no reservations.

I had my old job back, but I couldn't help but feeling helpless in that big house alone. I could not get used to the stability of my schedule at the hospital. I felt that going back to Port-au-Prince so soon would feel like going back to be with Sebastian. As Matt said to me the other day when I did not eat the food he brought me, "If you miss Port-au-Prince to a point you can't eat, you may as well go and stay there until you get it out of your system—if ever."

I didn't respond to that statement; I chose to go straight to bed instead of starting a spiteful argument where he would tell me that there was no hope or psychiatrist for me because I was so messed up, to which I would reply, "Well, at least I'm not a dropout sniffing after every girl who takes pity on me."

He would scream, and I would scream louder, and then he would tell me, "Oh, so now you can scream? How hilarious."

I would tell him, "Of course, because it was so damn good I couldn't find my voice." If he wanted to use my past to hurt me, I may as well use it to get right back at him.

Three weeks ago, I told him, "Oh wow, look who is using big words now." He was so angry that I thought he was going to kill me when he stared me down with his bloodshot eyes. But he left the house and did not come back till seven in the morning. Then he made breakfast, took out a plate for me, set it on the table with juice, and took a shower. He came in the room, kissed me while I faked sleeping, and left to work—or wherever he was going these days. Of course I left the food on the table just like he'd set it. Later he would come back and pull the Sebastian card, telling me he was sorry I missed Sebastian so much. I didn't know which place was worse, the earthquake or the hell Matt and I called home. He was like a ghost in the house. One minute I felt him standing behind me or sleeping by my side on the bed, and the next he disappeared before I could reach out to hold him.

Last night, he spent at least fifteen minutes with his arms around me, wrapped me underneath him while sleeping, I wanted to wake up to pee, but I couldn't because I knew if he realized he was holding me like that, he would probably move away from me like he was caught on fire. For fifteen minutes I lay there inert, and then I couldn't anymore. This man whom I loved so much and loved me was suffocating me. I could not breathe in the house without him telling me to go back to the paradise from which I'd come. I wanted to understand his pain, but I could not grasp the extent he was willing to go to hide it behind anger … or was it boiling, acidic hatred? I pulled myself from his arm and startled him from his profound sleep. He woke up and drew in his arms in defense, like someone was about to punch him. Yes, I did feel like it, but I settled for a pillow.

"D, stop that. I'm not kidding. Give me that pillow! What do you think you are doing?" he said.

I could not stop myself. I wanted to exhaust the bad blood out of both of us. I hit him until little balls of cotton started flying in the air almost like it was snowing. He used his hands to protect his eyes, but he just sat there and let me get it all out. When all I had in my hand was the fabric cover remains of the pillow, I let myself fall into bed face down. "I am tired, Matt. I am so tired. I can't do this anymore. If I told you I did not enjoy the week with Sebastian, I would be lying. Six months after we broke up, he was visiting, and Jessica told him I was in Port-au-Prince. He came to see me, and yes, I was happy to see him. Yes, we went dancing. Yes, we kissed and French kissed and neck kissed and shoulder kissed."

"Okay, okay, I get it. You guys did a lot of kissing," he shot back.

"But Matt, it just wasn't there. The thing is, I wanted to feel something with him. I wanted to prove to myself that maybe this fling was real. I wanted to deny my guilty conscience the pleasure of being wrong for breaking up my marriage for no reason. I wanted to find an excuse, anything to prove to myself that I made the right decision, that there was no other way around it. I felt nothing. I felt *nothing*, Matt. The only time I felt alive was when I was at the clinic helping those people. I felt accomplished, fulfilled, and at peace. It is not about you. It is not even about Sebastian. I just needed to find my purpose. You built us this huge house. You have your own business. I married the man I love, and I am a doctor, but in the back of my mind I always asked myself, 'Is that all there is?' There is that little something inside of me that is always empty. I felt empty even when I was the most happy and comfortable with you. Being here in this peaceful, picturesque mountain view house, with exotic music and most of all a great friend and husband—it's just not so peaceful for me, Matt. I don't feel all right. I love you, I really do, but I am afraid you could try to give me the whole world, and it would not be enough."

"I know."

"You know what?"

"It's been crushing me every day—that I am just not enough for you. All I want is to make you happy, but it makes me angry to realize that I am just not enough for you. I knew about Sebastian. I had a talk with him yesterday."

I was shocked. "What?"

"Long story."

I looked at Matt as he sat on the bed and avoided my eyes. Then I realized that hugging me in his sleep this morning was not a force of habit. He intentionally, purposely, consciously wrapped me under his arms to sleep.

"You thrive in chaos," he said. "When everything is falling apart, that is when you feel at most ease. You love helping these people not just because of your compassion, D. You feel comfortable in discomfited situation. And I am sorry that I cannot provide that for you."

Tears ran down my cheeks, and I let them slide down my lips. All these years I tried to understand why I felt so empty. I felt like I was in the presence of something sacred: the truth. I sighed and felt relieved of that mental burden. My body left me for a moment, and I felt like I was floating in the room like a happy cloud with a smiley face. When I felt the warmth of this familiar force pulling me back, I felt whole again, but this time with a fulfilled soul. He pressed my back against his chest and nearly squashed my shoulders. I nearly forgot that sweet force, that presence so resilient and pulling me back every time I thought I was falling to pieces.

He said, "How about instead of you taking care of others today, I take care of you?"

I smiled with tears flowing down on me like rivers, and I nodded with relief at what I thought I had lost. "Matt, can I ask you something?"

"Anything."

"Do you love her?"

"Who? Lila, my assistant? No. I only love you, D."

"How did you know who I was talking about?" I asked.

"Wild guess."

"If I were not here, would you stay with her?"

"I love only you, D. Whether you're here or far away, nothing will ever change that."

He sighed and kissed me. Then he let go of me with his left arm and affably scratched his head. I turned around, my chest pressing against his stomach, and I looked at his eyes. He smiled at me, combed through my hair with his finger, and made a messy ponytail before he kissed me again. That was how I knew.

I was not enough, either. And an angel somehow was gradually sharing a quarter of my space. I was in the scenario of "Mrs. Wrong," and love was the irrepressible chain keeping this man in my net. He was a prisoner who did not want his freedom, a near-death patient who did not want to be treated. That was who I saw in my bed that morning. His will, his strength, and his warmth were holding on to me, but his eyes were drowning in secret wishes of a different life, a different marriage, a different family, a different home, a different type of argument … a different wife.

He ran a hot bath, gently took my hands, and led me to the bathtub. He took my sweaty camisole off and slid off my panties like we were in ancient times and I was a queen being prepped to meet her king. He stepped in the water with his underwear as if to tell himself this bath was solely for me. When I sat in front of him, with my buttocks pressing against his crotch, something told me that it was a lie. He took the sponge and tenderly erased each kiss he placed on my neck, my arms, and my shoulders. When he glided the wet, soapy sponge between my breasts, I closed my eyes and leaned my head back on his right shoulder. I decided to clear my head in the silence and play in my head the first song I could think of, but what I really heard was the rhythm of his heart on my spine; his soothing, dancing breath surrounding my neck; and the water succumbing to any movement he made.

That was supposed to be my moment. I felt he was the king controlling every movement in the atmosphere. I felt like even the breeze that sneaked its way through the doors was part of his plan. He showered my head with a sponge full of warm water, and the river glided all the way down my waist. He let go of the sponge, and squeezed my thighs, and slid his fingers back to my birthmark. He vacationed there like he was trying to remember what it looked like. He drew every bone in my ribs and broadened his brush when he reached my nipples, which hardened under his artistic sense. He drew their circle and massaged the surrounding nerves. He always joked that God had created my breast to be just enough to fill his palms. When he touched me there, I joined my hands to his and massaged his pectorals with my shoulders.

Under the hot rain of this pleasurable shower, we rinsed the bubbles off our skin. I faced him and slid his underwear off. I stayed on my knees, taking his strength away from him while he massaged every inch of my hair.

When we rinsed off, he bit my ear and whispered, "You are inconceivable."

My strength left me when he pushed me on the bed and pulled off my towel. He flipped me over on my belly but raised me by the shoulders, putting me on my knees. He held my neck and caressed my waist. I leaned back, offering my whole to him. He abandoned my neck to work on my nipples. When his finger reached inside of me, I was already there. I felt him on my posterior like he had never surrendered to me in the bathroom. He was my king, and I was a willing damsel. I leaned on my belly and let him take me wherever he intended to go. His finger, replaced, proceeded to press on my waist or massage my shoulder blade in order to bring me closer to him. I melted into him like we were one body with different souls emerging from the flames of the instant. He was fully mine, and I was fully his. His sweat dropped on me like heavy rain melting into my skin, running in my blood and drawing out the little strength I had left in me like a strong drug. My eyes turned blind, and my ears could hear his faint moans from far away. It was like being the passenger to a driver speeding his car up to infinite: I could feel the rush without the effort. My mind was blank, and my soul was in a trance.

When he leaned on me and kissed me, I knew that it was not a dream and that this presence was real. He moved me through hours of infinite, and we explored the teaching of dear Kama Sutra until our ligaments were thirsty for a siesta.

Matt sat down on the bed, leaned against the cold wall, and pulled my weak body against him. "I love you, damn it."

We laughed with the remainder of our beings, and it echoed off the walls. I kissed him and wiped the sweat off his face. We laughed until a drop of tear ran down his eyes, which he quickly and swiftly wiped it like it was his sweat. I saw it and kissed it. "I love you more than you can imagine, Matt."

Chapter 15

Waking up to a beautiful morning after a delightful yesterday was the best feeling in the world. I stretched my arms, yawned deliberately, and noticed that Matt was not in bed. I could hear his voice on the phone from the balcony. When he saw me coming, he started the process of his good-bye to the person, and then he smiled and stretched out his arm so I could wrap myself in his embrace. I placed a tender kiss on his chest and raised my head to implore him with my eyes to say good-bye. The rooster from the village sang its second *cocoriquo!*

Matt said good-bye and put the phone in his pocket, and the phone pulled his shorts down a little. I touched his stomach and felt that Matt had lost the vigor of his muscles a little. "Is it me, or did you lose weight?" I asked.

"Yeah, I lost a few pounds over the past few months."

I did not ask anything else. "Come on, let's go make breakfast." I pulled his arms and put them over my shoulders, and we made our way downstairs to the kitchen. I handed him the sheet that I'd folded around my body, and I caught his eyes staring at my bare breasts like he'd never seen them before.

"Are you going to cook wearing nothing but your panties?" he asked.

"Is there a problem?"

"Ca alors!" He rubbed his chin and devoured me from head to toe.

"Someone would think you've never seen a naked woman before," I teased.

"Well, it's been a long time since I've seen you walking around the house like that. A very long time."

"I see."

He leaned on the counter, watching my every move in the kitchen without saying another word. At first I felt uncomfortable, but then something came over me. I leaned over to look for things in the lowest compartment in the fridge and took them out one by one. I whisked the eggs more than I had to. I massaged the juice out of the oranges. When I was frying the omelet, I comfortably rested my other hand on my hips, and then I flipped the omelet with the long fork … and most of it ended up on the floor. When I heard the suffocating laughter behind me, I started laughing. too. Matt was laughing so hard that I felt embarrassed, but he approached me, moved the pan, turned off the stove, and took the fork from my hands. He grabbed my lips with such unexpected passion. I closed my eyes and enjoyed the mint flavor from his tongue. The next thing I knew, I was up in the air with my back resting on the cold granite where his plate was going to be. His warmth invaded my blood, and I savored every minute of this trip. Besides the omelet on the floor, a few slices of bread, and the orange juice, there was nothing else for breakfast, but that was the least of my worries. As far as I was concerned, we could worry about that later … much later.

I walked on the street, and I found that a lot had changed since I'd left. The butcher had a café that turned into a Fritay bar at night. In the morning, he had hot coffee, chocolate, and even thé citronelle or gingembre around December, along with hot fresh croissants or cabiche, bananas, roasted peanuts, and boiled eggs—almost everything for a good, healthy breakfast. Then after 6:00 PM, he had any fried food one wanted to eat, from fish to pork to Akra to dumplings. He had a lot of clients, and I was so shocked to see that he was doing it all by himself with the help of a young girl he'd sent for from Port-Magot. I did not know the butcher could cook. It was a surprise!

When he saw Matt, he came outside and handed him a brown bag with two big cups of black coffee. One of the clients screamed, "Ki bagay patipri sa, mwen te la anvan misye sa!"[6] Then everybody else joined in, screaming how they had been waiting in line for hours now, and that was bad customer service.

Then the butcher turned around and said at the top of his voice, "Si se pat pou misye sa, nou pa tap menm jwenn lin pou nou kanpe vin achte."[7] He added, "No matter how many hours everybody else has been waiting, this guy is always going to be served first, because Matt is the reason I am not begging in the streets right now." Then people applauded and waved to Matt.

One guy still insisted, "Mwen pa bezwen tande tout rablabla sa yo, banm café m voyem ale lakay mwen, madanm nan ap tann mwen."[8]

---

[6] "What is this nonsense! I was here first."

[7] "If it were not for this man, you would not even find a line to stand in."

[8] "I don't need to hear all this jabbering. Give me my coffee and send me home, because my wife is waiting for me."

I laughed and told Matt we should probably leave before that guy threw his pot at us. The butcher gave me a big hug and welcomed me back. I hadn't seen him since I came back. He said something about not having time to come see us right now, but he would pay a visit next weekend. The noise started to be unbearable, and he went back in before they ate the young girl inside alive.

"Wow! Look at you, Mr. Popular."

"Well, I don't know about being popular. I simply helped a friend in need. His butchery was doing poorly, and he owed so many people money. I helped him pay them off, and I loaned him some money to open this little thing."

"'This little thing'? Did you see how many people were waiting in line? He's going to need to hire people to help him or send for every far-away cousin and sister he has in the province to help him!"

We both laughed at my last comment. I looked into Matt's eyes and saw true happiness for the first time since I'd been back. I tightened my grip around his waist, and he squeezed my shoulders. It was one of those moments one wished would last an eternity.